The world is in peril.

An ancient evil is rising from beneath Erdas, and we need YOU to help stop it.

Claim your spirit animal and join the adventure now:

1. Go to scholastic.com/spiritanimals.

2. Log in to create your character and choose your own spirit animal.

3. Have your book ready and enter the code below to unlock the adventure.

Your code: N4RMFC6X3M

By the Four Fallen,
The Greencloaks

I will help rescue
your spirit animal,
or die trying.

TALES OF THE

FALLEN BEASTS

TALES OF THE
FALLEN BEASTS

BRANDON MULL

Emily Seife ⬩ Nick Eliopulos

Gavin Brown ⬩ Billy Merrell

SCHOLASTIC INC.

Library of Congress Control Number: 2015956412

ISBN 978-0-545-90138-3
10 9 8 7 6 5 4 3 2 1   16 17 18 19 20

Book design by Charice Silverman
Map illustration by Michael Walton

Library edition, March 2016

Printed in the U.S.A.   23

Scholastic US: 557 Broadway • New York, NY 10012
Scholastic Canada: 604 King Street West • Toronto, ON M5V 1E1
Scholastic New Zealand Limited: Private Bag 94407 • Greenmount, Manukau 2141
Scholastic UK Ltd.: Euston House • 24 Eversholt Street • London NW1 1DB

HALAWIR

UNLEASHED

By Emily Seife

THERE WAS A TREMENDOUS BRILLIANCE, LIKE A BLINDFOLD had just been pulled away from his eyes, and for a moment Halawir felt nothing but the sting of too much light everywhere. He was consumed by a purple radiance, the whole world like the penumbra of the sun.

And then the rest of his body caught up to his eyes. He was joyfully aware of the wind in his feathers. He could taste the salt spray and smell the raw, endless sea pulsing below him. He heard the rush of the air as it parted to make room for his body.

He was soaring.

He pumped his wide wings up and down, enjoying the way they pushed the air around, currents tense and smooth as water, the tips of his wings brushing lightly against the sky. He stretched them out to their fullest span, nearly seven feet, so that he could see the sun glinting on the blue and gray of the feathers under his wings.

Halawir let out an exultant scream.

He was a Great Beast, and king of these skies.

Fast and focused, majestic wings now flush against his body, Halawir reached the apex of his flight and turned to dive down. A seagull crossed his line of vision, and he lunged at it playfully.

Of course, the seagull didn't know that Halawir was simply feeling out his strength—it assumed it was destined to be dinner. It flapped away as fast as it could, squawking wildly. Halawir's eyes squinted in an avian smile. If he were in the mood to hunt, that seagull wouldn't have a chance. But he let the bird go.

Now he saw an ocean of Erdas spread out below him. He still didn't know where he was, just that it was good to be here at all—to be back.

He zipped down farther still, skimming along the surface of the foamy sea—following the curves and crests of the waves but never getting wet—then up over a sea trader's sleek boat—

The next moment, a heavy net fell over his head. His wings tangled up in the rope and he came crashing down, landing on a hard surface with an undignified thud. He tried flapping his wings, squirming to get free of the net, but he only got more and more ensnared. Casting his eyes about wildly, Halawir could see that he was on the deck of the boat. Well-worn wooden planks slid beneath his talons as he scrambled to get his footing back.

"You got him!" exclaimed a high voice, followed by footsteps running toward him. "I can't believe it! He's incredible."

It sounded like a child. Halawir's panic threatened to overwhelm him, but as the pumping in his heart subsided, he could see the young girl crouched next to him. She looked to be about eleven. Her skin was brown and her hair was pale, as if the sun had both toasted and bleached her.

A deeper voice spoke. It was a man dressed simply but neatly, with the same dark skin as the girl. "Cordalles, you did it! You've summoned a spirit animal!" The man paused, and Halawir could hear him trying to control the pride in his voice. "A bird is the perfect creature for a seafarer like you."

"That's not just a *bird*," snapped the woman standing next to him. "Did you see its wingspan? Look at its hooked beak. It's an eagle, Imari."

"An eagle?" said the girl, Cordalles. Halawir turned his yellow eyes to peer at her. "It can't be an eagle," the girl continued. "Everyone knows that you can't summon an eagle as a spirit animal, because Halawir—" She bit off the end of her sentence.

"Halawir," the man echoed. "The Great Beast?"

"The *betrayer*," said the woman sourly.

"This can't be him," the girl said, but Halawir could hear the doubt in her voice. She didn't sound all that happy. Well, that made two of them.

Cordalles craned her neck to get a better look at his face through the net. Halawir pumped his massive wings again in protest, but the heavy net didn't allow him to gain any traction in the air. He let out a screech of rage. It was absurd to be kept trapped by a bunch of seafaring nobodies who probably couldn't even spot a fish flashing beneath the waves from three hundred meters away.

Halawir had come close to ruling all of Erdas alongside Kovo and Gerathon. He had held the shining talismans in his talons, had seen the arrogant Greencloaks run screaming from their silly castle. The war had turned against him and his allies in the end, but Halawir knew what it was to be one of the mightiest creatures on the face of Erdas. He knew what it was to make people tremble. And now—

He narrowed his yellow eyes at the girl to show that they were not friends, that they could never be friends. But she was ignoring that very clear signal. In fact, she reached her pointer finger out to lightly touch one of the blue-gray feathers under his mighty wings.

"He is beautiful," she said.

"Careful, Cordalles," the girl's mother warned, and rightfully so.

Halawir would certainly have pulled away, if he could. Would have happily clawed her eyes out, if he could. But he was immobilized, with no choice but to wait as she ran the tip of her finger along the length of his feathers, as if he were some little fluffy-headed chick, too young and weak and stupid to know how to fly.

Still, as she stroked his glossy feathers, he felt himself weakening. It was like some tiny yellow chick *was* there inside him, cracking out of the shell of his heart and leaning in toward Cordalles.

It surprised and scared him, the tentative feeling of connection between them. The hours the girl spent at the top of the boat's rigging, the sea flying by her and the wind whipping her hair into a froth, left a scent of the sky on her. That was something they shared. He sensed that she loved the feel of the wind in her face, like he did.

But he didn't like this weak spot in himself. She was holding him prisoner.

That could not be forgiven.

He would not be some girl's spirit animal, dependent on her whim. He would not subject himself to the passive state. Maybe that was fine for slow-moving Jhi, or a more common creature, but not him.

Halawir used the power of his strong will to turn himself away from the spark of their bond. He would ignore it until, like any burning ember with no fuel, it would fade out and die.

As he had sat there like a dumb cow, dazed by the touch of the girl's finger, the older woman had been approaching. Now, all of a sudden, she reached under the net and pulled on Halawir's leg.

Again, he fought, the sudden softness forgotten, this undesirable intimacy stirring him to intense anger. He thrashed his wings and neck and legs, but she had him, she had his delicate leg. He tensed his talons, hoping for at least one good scratch on her tough hide, and when that didn't work he curved his body around and dove in with his beak for a peck. He tasted blood. She screeched and pulled away, but not before she had slipped a little knotted rope up over his foot and tightened it around his leg.

"That beast attacked me!" The woman brandished her arm in front of her. Halawir saw the gouge his beak had made in her fleshy forearm. Good.

"Mother!" the girl cried. "Are you okay? I'm so sorry! I didn't know he would–Halawir, how could you do that?"

"I'm fine. At least I got the leash on so we can get him under control." The mother's mouth twisted into a grim smile and she handed the other end of the rope to the girl. Then together, the woman and the man untangled the net and lifted it away from Halawir.

The second it was gone, he took off into the sky.

He wasn't stupid; some part of his mind remembered that he was leashed, but his instincts were connected directly to his muscles, and he reacted long before his mind was able to chime in with some helpful advice. His heart soared and his wings followed, the instinct alive and immediate. Like an arrow shot into the sky, he took off–until he reached the end of the cord.

It yanked back on his leg, hard, and he boomeranged down in a tumble of feathers and fury onto the deck.

"Shhh," said the girl, his captor, the other end of the rope twisted around her wrist. "Calm down."

Calm down.

He was on a leash like a groveling *pet*, and she thought he was going to roll over and play along?

She looked up at the adults. "Isn't he supposed to feel a bond with me?"

"It's natural, when a spirit animal is first called, for the bond to be weak," answered her mother. "It's something that both partners must work on and cultivate. Something that the two will strengthen over the years. Usually."

Halawir let out a cackling laugh and his feathers raised like hackles. He wouldn't be working to strengthen this bond. He had no interest in becoming any closer with a sniveling child. He'd had enough bad experiences with children already. He shook out his wings, brushing off the memory of Meilin, Abeke, Rollan, and Conor. Those baby Greencloaks who had cost him, well, everything.

"Okay, we'll work on it," Cordalles said, only the hint of a question in her voice. "I'm sure that once we spend time together our bond will feel more, um . . ." She coughed. "I'm sure there's lots we can learn from each other, anyway. Lots he can teach me." Her voice perked up with newfound enthusiasm. "Maybe soon I'll be running across the deck of the boat as fast as though I had wings."

Her father smiled. "Or maybe you could be our new lookout, once you have eyesight as powerful as an eagle's. Relieve Bao of his night watch."

"Yes!" Cordalles crowed. "And I'll—"

"One step at a time, little sparrow," her mother said, placing her hand firmly on Cordalles's shoulder.

"You'll see," Cordalles said. She shrugged the hand

back off. "And with Halawir to look out for me, you'll let me go off on my own when we dock, maybe? Since he'll be there to protect me. We'll start working on strengthening our bond right away, won't we, Halawir?"

It was a clear question that demanded a clear answer.

He unfolded his wings and gave one powerful beat to launch himself up. Hovering on the softest air current, he felt himself relax into the air. Floating lightly at the end of his tether, he positioned himself directly above Cordalles. He could see her parents standing close by her, and the ship's crew looking on curiously from around the deck.

Then he loosened his bowels and pooped on her head.

An hour later, Halawir was sitting on a small perch in a cramped bunk in the depths of the boat. He had to hunch his shoulders up around his neck to fit his bulk inside the tiny room. There was a low ceiling that sloped up from an even lower wall. Only one round porthole showed a glimpse of the outdoors: a swinging view that flashed between sea and sky, sea and sky. Cordalles had just finished washing her hair in a bucket and was toweling it dry in the opposite corner of the room, as far away from Halawir as she could get, which wasn't very far at all.

"I didn't know Great Beasts had such great senses of humor," Cordalles said, not laughing.

Halawir was aware that his form of objection had

not been the most *dignified*, unfortunately. But in this instance, he hadn't felt he'd had any avenues of complaint open to him other than this silent protest.

He could tell that Cordalles and her parents didn't trust him. Well, that made them and every other human on the planet. His reputation was, at the moment, much more powerful than he was.

She took a deep breath. "You are my spirit animal, you know. I didn't choose this any more than you did, but here you are. You're as bonded to me as I am to you, so we should really make the best of it. Trust each other, and all that. Okay?"

She stuck her left arm out in front of her.

Halawir stared at her blankly. Was this some strange seafarer's friendship ritual? No, thanks.

Then, with a start, he realized that she was holding out her arm for him to transform into a tattoo on her skin, the passive form of a spirit animal. Was she out of her mind? He let out a harsh cry of derision. She was a fool and had learned nothing about him if she thought that he would willingly submit himself to her.

He turned his back to her haughtily and closed his eyes, but she kept talking to him.

"You know my parents don't like you. They don't trust you at all. To tell you the truth, they don't trust me much, either." She sighed. "Whenever we dock, they never let me go off on my own to look around. We visit some of the finest cities in the world, all the largest ports in Erdas, and they never let me out of their sight! So, if it makes you feel any better, I know what it feels like not to be trusted."

Halawir wished he could shut his ears as well as his eyes. For now he was a prisoner, stuck here in these oppressive quarters out in the middle of the ocean, but soon he would be free of these humans and their petty quarrels and concerns.

At least he wasn't in danger at the moment. He would rest. Gather his strength. As soon as they approached land, he would make his escape.

Halawir kept his eyes firmly shut to the world until, at long last, he heard footsteps. A moment later, Cordalles's mother squeezed through the low door to the room. She perched on the bunk next to her daughter and ran her fingers through the girl's wet hair.

"I've been talking to your father," she said in a low voice, as though Halawir couldn't hear if she whispered. "We're not quite sure what to do with this . . . with your . . . with Halawir."

"What do you mean?" Cordalles said.

"Well, it's unheard of to summon a Great Beast, except for the four heroes who stopped the Conquerors. We've spoken to all the sailors on the ship, but no one's got a clue what it means, or what to do with him. We're in luck, though. We're heading through the Strait of Gibral toward Amaya, which means that Greenhaven, the home of the Greencloaks, will be pretty much on our way. Your father and I think we should stop there. Perhaps the Greencloaks will be able to give us some guidance. They spend their lives dealing with matters of these bonds. Someone there will certainly know what to do with it—with him."

Cordalles furrowed her brow. "There's nothing *to* do. He's my spirit animal. Just like Juno has Freelam, or Bao has—"

"My sweet seagull, you must see that it's not the same. This bird was one of the masterminds of the Devourer Wars. He's smaller now, so I know it's hard to believe, but he was once so huge that the Devourer rode through the skies on his back. This is the creature whose schemes and tricks cost thousands of lives. He even betrayed his fellow Great Beasts. I'm not sure that's exactly the type of animal you want as your cabinmate."

"We have a bond, though," Cordalles said. "I can *definitely* feel it."

Halawir almost choked. She was clearly lying through her teeth to her mother. He couldn't help admiring her almost a little; she was very convincing.

He must have made a strange noise, because Cordalles's mother started. Halawir wondered if she realized that he could understand every word she was saying.

She pulled Cordalles into her arms. "Just because you love birds doesn't mean they're all your friends. Look, I'm not saying you'll need to be separated from him permanently. I just think we should get some advice from the Greencloaks, is all. It's only a few days' sailing out of our way. We've informed the crew of the slight change in route. They're happy to be getting the extra pay." She leaned down and kissed the girl on the top of her head. "Let your father and I decide what's best for you, my sparrow."

Cordalles shrugged her mother off. She straightened her narrow shoulders and looked right at Halawir. "You wouldn't betray me, would you? You can feel that there's something—something connecting us?"

Halawir closed his eyes against the intensity of her gaze.

They were taking him to Greenhaven, the home of his enemies.

For the very first time, he felt thankful that fate had brought him this girl.

He would finally have a chance for revenge.

Just then, the sack came down over his head.

Cordalles's mother tossed him unceremoniously into a windowless cabin even smaller—if such a thing was possible—than the one Cordalles had originally brought him to.

She stood watch from a safe distance while a burly sailor tied his leash to a post and placed bowls of water and dried meat near him.

Finally, the sailor left the room, giving one last suspicious glance to Halawir as he left, and the woman smiled in faux apology.

"I know you'll understand," she said. "I can't let my daughter become too attached to you. It's for her own good. Yours too, probably. What if a true bond developed? It would be all the worse when we would eventually have to separate you two. Because my daughter is *not* going to spend her life with a traitor as her spirit animal. She deserves better than that." Saliva flew from her lips as she spat the last words at him. Perhaps she was trying to shame him, but Halawir didn't care about that at all. "We'll leave you with the Greencloaks," she continued. "You can be their problem."

So she'd been lying, too. Halawir couldn't care less about being separated from Cordalles, either. The only thing that mattered to him was that the ship continued on its course toward Greenhaven.

The woman left the room. He could hear the sound of the door locking behind her, followed by running feet, and then, faintly, the sound of someone crying. He perked up his ears. Eagles were known for their keen eyesight, but his hearing wasn't bad, either.

"–have to let me in." It was Cordalles, sobbing and pleading with her mother. "I'm telling you, he'll listen to me. Don't you trust me at *all*?"

"It's not you I don't trust."

"You never let me do anything!"

Then the deeper voice of the father: "Cordalles, listen to your mother. She's protecting you for your own good. This is only temporary, until we hear what the Greencloaks have to say. Then we can use their training and wisdom to make sure your bond with Halawir is a good one."

Footsteps, and the crying grew fainter.

He was alone.

Day after day passed, and the only thing Halawir learned about boats was that life on board was interminably slow.

The light that snuck under the door frame faded and grew and faded again. The same sailor came with food day after day, but he never took Halawir out, or even made eye contact or spoke to the bird.

Awake and asleep, Halawir dreamed of freedom. He pictured the day when Cordalles would take him on shore to the Greencloak castle. They would never let him stay with her—but who knows what they *would* want to do with him? Throw him into another prison, probably.

No, he needed to break away before Lenori and the other Greencloaks realized who he was.... Maybe he would make his escape as they walked onto land. He could startle Cordalles, make her drop him. Or should he wait until he was inside the castle, among his enemies, poised for revenge? The plan changed every time he thought about it. The only constant was his hunger for freedom.

Then one day, the dawn brought a tremendous amount of noise and excitement. Halawir could hear the sailors running around the deck, readying the boat, hauling ropes—he tried to peer through the crack in the door to see what was going on, but it was impossible to make anything out.

It was only when the endless forward motion of the boat suddenly stopped that he realized they had reached a port. Was this Greenhaven? Had they gotten there already? The deadly fog of monotony suddenly lifted from his brain, and he perked up. At any moment, Cordalles or her mother would show up to bring him out of his prison and take him to the Greencloaks!

He waited impatiently. He could hear the crew singing and laughing as they raced down the gangplank to shore, but still, no one came for him.

Then the deck quieted down.

What had happened? Why had they left him behind? This was not part of any of his hundreds of plans. What now?

Despair tore through him. He would never be free of this family, this boat, this room. He picked up the water dish with his talons and hurled it across the room. It hit the far wall with a clang, water splashing everywhere.

Then Halawir heard a careful key in the lock. The sailor in charge of feeding him must have been left on board to keep watch. But it was not the usual time for food, and the sound was softer and more hesitant than usual.

The door creaked open, and Cordalles threw herself around the edge.

"They didn't take me with them!" She stared at him with wide eyes, as though she expected him to know what she was talking about.

He cocked his head to the side. After so many days in isolation, he had to admit that he was the slightest bit pleased to see her.

"We stopped at a port to drop off some cargo. A

quick stop." Halawir felt a rush of relief. They weren't at Greenhaven yet after all. There was still hope. He perked up, fluffing his feathers.

Cordalles smiled, noticing his attention, before remembering why she'd stormed in. "My parents wouldn't even let me off the boat!" She picked up Halawir's battered water dish and threw it at a wall, just as he had. "I thought that now that I've summoned a spirit animal they'd have a little more confidence in me, let me explore on my own—and instead they're worse than ever! They don't even let me off the boat!" She buried her head in her hands for a minute. "Well, we'll show them, won't we? We really have to prove ourselves now."

She stood up. Her cheeks were flushed. "I stole the spare key! Now I can come see you whenever I want. And I will. I'm sorry that I was so . . . so scared. That I didn't come see you before.

"There's only one more stop before Greenhaven. We'll be docking at Soussia for an afternoon, and I'm going to prove to them that we can do just fine on our own. By the time we get to Greenhaven, we'll be able to show the Greencloaks that we really do have a bond. That they can trust both of us."

There was a distant thud—the sound of new cargo being loaded into the steerage.

"I have to go," Cordalles whispered. "But I'll be back."

The next night, back out on the ocean, she kept her promise, coming to visit after everyone was asleep but the few night watchmen.

"Are you there?" she whispered. "I didn't dare light a candle."

Halawir could see perfectly at night, so he watched her fumbling blindly with the door while her eyes adjusted to the deeper darkness of the cabin. She pressed her back against the wall and slid down to the floor. He could see that her pupils were completely dilated, little black holes in the night. Cordalles pulled a bag off her arm and rummaged around inside.

"If I'm going to get them to trust us, I have to be sure I can trust you," she said. "Then, at our next stop, we'll sneak off the boat together. I've started working on something. I'm almost done. Then we can get you outside again."

That got his attention immediately.

She took out a pair of tiny leather anklets, and then pulled out a partially cut piece of leather.

He realized she had been making him a set of jesses, the traditional leash used for trained hawks. It was a strap cut from leather, used for keeping hawks—or Great Eagles, in this case—from flying away.

Jess, he thought. It sounded like *jest*, like something fun. In fact, it was just the opposite. But if it was a step toward his freedom . . .

It would be more comfortable, he supposed, than the rough piece of rope the mother had fastened to his ankle his first day on the boat. But he was not interested in analyzing the comfort levels of the tools of his imprisonment. He was more focused on getting free.

"I'd rather not use the jess at all, you know," Cordalles said, half to him, half to herself. "But"—and she looked up at him sharply—"I'm not entirely sure that you won't fly away the second I let you off the leash."

He couldn't believe she was even debating the question. Of *course* he would fly away the second he was let free.

"Soon," she continued, "you'll come to trust me. You'll feel our bond stronger—and then you can fly anywhere you want, because I'll know you'll come back. Till then, we'll have to make do with this."

She turned her concentration to the leather that she'd smoothed out on the floor in front of her. Cordalles picked up her knife and made a long, precise slice close to the edge of the piece of leather. It created a thin strap.

"Looks good, right?" She held it up for Halawir to see. He dropped his eyelids, hoping she'd be smart enough to realize that he had no interest in the project. It was the end result—flying free—that interested him.

When Cordalles had finished trimming and smoothing and attaching the leather pieces, she approached him carefully. He decided to let her. The more she believed in their bond, the better chance he had at being let free. He could make his escape at Soussia, and then fly to Greenhaven on his own, once he was prepared. . . .

Cordalles attached the anklet to him and held the end of the jess in her hand.

"Your chariot, sir," she said, holding out her arm.

She intended her statement as a joke, but Halawir never joked. And any opportunity for her to serve him was one he would take. He hopped onto her arm and gripped it tightly with his talons, so that she could carry him out to the deck. He could feel the muscles in her arm straining under his solid weight.

Cordalles softly tiptoed out of the cabin. It opened onto one of the lower decks. She must have made sure the night watchman would be stationed elsewhere; this area of the deck was quiet and deserted.

All around them, from horizon to horizon, stars glittered madly, like droplets of water shaken off by a shivering moon. Halawir could see the tiny faraway lights vibrating in the sky.

Out in the clean ocean air on deck, he could finally breathe again. The cramped quarters had truly started to drive him crazy. He rolled his neck, stretching out his muscles. The ship heaved and pitched on the choppy waves. The salt air smelled like freedom.

Halawir's heart soared.

Cordalles fed out the leash so that Halawir could fly through the air above the boat, stretching his wings and flexing his brawny chest. Despite his resentment, he was not going to pass up the opportunity to move.

When he finally returned to her arm, Cordalles's smile was as wide as the crescent moon above them.

"See?" she whispered. "We can be good partners. We'll keep doing this, so that when we get to Soussia, we can go off, maybe do a trade of our own. Mother and Father will have to see the value of our bond after that. Then, at Greenhaven, we can show everyone how well we work together. Mother promised me that the Greencloaks would explain all the rules of a bond with a Great Beast."

He stared at her unblinkingly. If he knew anything from his time on earth, it was that rules were made so that the weak would feel safe and protected, so they could believe there was something bigger and stronger watching over them. That was a lie.

The truth, Halawir knew, was that rules were the way the clever gained power—by breaking them.

Yes, this little sea noodle had summoned him, somehow. But they were no more bound to each other than he was bound to this ship. They were simply thrown together momentarily. He would break away, smashing whatever bond she imagined existed, the first chance he got. And he would never look back.

Night after night, Cordalles snuck Halawir out and flew him.

He began to become accustomed to her little habits. If she played with her hair, he could tell that she was nervous, and he wouldn't fly so far.

And if she raised her hand above her head, he knew it meant that their time was up, and he would return to perch on her arm or shoulder.

She was teaching him to work with her, and he was teaching her that he could be trusted.

Then one morning, a shout from the rigging shook him out of his daydreams.

"Land ahead!"

Halawir flew to a little knot he'd discovered in the wooden wall. It gave him a peephole to the outdoors.

The usually calm deck was transformed. All the sailors had dropped whatever task they'd been doing and emerged into the sunlight. Boys were running around, scuttling up and down the masts, adjusting the sails, prepping the anchor, and tightening lines.

Halawir imagined that at the top of the tallest mast, one boy clung on with one hand, holding a long spyglass in the other. But with his sharp eyes, Halawir could clearly see what the boy had probably needed to use the telescope to spot. Right at the horizon line was a sliver of land—a port city.

Cordalles had told him that they'd be stopping soon to off-load some goods, make some trades, and restock their food supplies. One last stop before Greenhaven.

Everything was bustle and frenzy as they made ready to dock, but Halawir was left, forgotten, in the gloom of his prison. The sailor who usually brought his food didn't even remember to come feed him.

As the boat pulled into port, Halawir watched through the knot as the sky filled with seagulls eager to see what treats—what fish—this new vessel might have to offer. They swooped through the sky above him. Stupid, slow birds. If he was freed, Halawir knew, he could accelerate up above them, take in their positions before they had time to react, and then drop like a stone, talons outstretched, grabbing one of them tightly and tearing it from limb to limb—

He sighed and dropped down to the floor, heavy with boredom.

Gradually, the cries of the sailors thinned out. He could hear their feet running down the gangplank as the crew took to shore for a day of fun. Cordalles's parents would be off trading their goods. The ship stood empty.

This, he knew, was when she'd come for him.

The door swung open.

Cordalles stood there with a tremendous smile plastered across her face. Halawir would have laughed at how pleased with herself she appeared, except that he'd never felt so excited to see anyone in his whole life.

Despite himself, he leaped up into the air and onto her arm in greeting.

She smoothed his ruffled feathers down and even chucked him under the chin playfully.

"Are you ready?" she asked. "Mother and Father have gone. There's barely anyone left on board. I gave Zak a gold coin not to notice if we slip away for just a little while. I have a fun plan." Her gleeful smile shone in the small room.

She was wearing a long dark cloak, and she pulled it over her arm so that Halawir was concealed as they left the ship.

As soon as they reached land, she flung the garment away.

"Ta-da!" she cried happily. "I'll tell you what we're going to do. What could be better than a new green robe to wear when we visit the Greencloaks? I know the man Mother and Father always visit for new robes.

We'll find his stall and get a fine green robe to wear. Imagine the look on their faces when I show up with a new green cloak, and you on my arm, as calm as can be."

Cordalles blended into the crowd. They were surrounded by throngs of people. Halawir balanced lightly on her arm and surveyed the bustling port of Soussia. Like every port city he'd ever seen—except during times of war—the docks were bursting with activity. Sailors and passengers flooded off leisure boats and shipping vessels.

The people were dressed in everything from dirty rags to the richest robes. The styles ranged from the severe jackets of Eura to the colorful robes of Nilo. Drivers with carts and horses jostled each other to get closest to the richest passengers with the most luggage. Porters with stooped backs took remarkably quick steps under the heavy burdens of trunks and bags. Farther inland, Halawir could see stands displaying fruits and meats and spices and teas. Halawir fed off the noise and energy of the city, but as Cordalles made her way through the winding streets, he started to feel as though something was not quite right.

He felt almost as though someone was watching them. It was a silly thing to think, because of course many eyes were on them. A cheerful old woman nodded in their direction as they passed, wishing them a good morning. A man with a sparrow spirit animal flinched when he saw them and darted away across the street. A gaggle of little kids followed Cordalles for a moment, trying to guess where she was from. There were thousands of eyes in this city, and everyone was sizing each other up, and then moving right along.

Still, Halawir couldn't escape the feeling of paranoia that had threaded its way through him.

When he caught sight of a man in a dark tunic turning a corner up ahead, he felt as though he'd found the source of his anxiety, though he couldn't tell why. A moment later, the man disappeared from sight.

A few blocks later, he thought he spotted the man's dark tunic and close-cropped dark hair again. Of course, it could have been anyone. There were thousands of men in dark robes making their way through this port city.

Halawir tightened the grip of his talons around Cordalles's glove, determined to enjoy their outing and ignore his instincts.

Still, when Halawir and Cordalles finally reached the garment district, an area where the street opened up into a central square, he couldn't resist checking all the alley exits to make sure the man was not trailing them.

Nothing.

He breathed a sigh of relief as Cordalles, oblivious, surveyed the square. It was full of booths. Some were piled with bolts of cloth of all colors, for those who wanted to create their own clothes. Some sold delicately stitched dresses, for those with money to spare. There were puffy coats and thin stockings and everything in between.

Cordalles clearly wasn't prepared for quite so many stalls.

"I'll ask someone where we can find Lukasz," she said.

She looked around, hesitant. Halawir could tell that she wanted to find someone nonthreatening who she could approach for help. He realized that many of the people around them would look worldly and intimidating to a girl accustomed to the contained universe of a boat. There was a Zhongese soldier, a bedraggled beggar, a haughty-looking Niloan. . . .

"She looks friendly!" Cordalles whispered at last. She started walking toward a Zhongese girl who was browsing at a stand under the colonnade that sold pretty embroidered cloths.

The girl was about Cordalles's age but looked more mature, somehow. She was lovely, with long dark hair and tan skin, and dressed in the clothes of someone well-off. Halawir guessed that she was the daughter of one of the city's prosperous merchants, sent out to buy something for a last-minute dinner party.

"Excuse me," said Cordalles, tapping the girl on her shoulder. "I'm looking for the robe trader named Lukasz. Do you know where his stall is?"

The girl turned around. Up close, her face was plainer than he'd thought at first. But when her lips curled into a smile, she looked a little like a hungry cat.

"Yes, of course," she said. Her voice was as smooth and luxurious as a silk robe. Only the slightest trace of a southern Zhongese accent hung on her words, like the faint scent of cardamom on a tablecloth at the end of a rich meal. "Everyone knows where Lukasz's stall is; he is one of the finest craftsmen in the city. You know you'll be getting good quality when you buy from him."

"That's his reputation," said Cordalles. "It's why my parents always like to trade with him when we're in town."

"Your parents must be smart people. Are they here with you?"

"Oh yes, but they're back at the port, selling our goods. We're sea traders." Cordalles gestured at her sail-cloth dress. "As you can see. That's why I'm here to pick up some new robes for our season on shore."

"Of course!" The girl seemed to remember the reason for their conversation. "I'm sorry for keeping you! It's just always interesting to talk to people from other places. You're lucky to be able to travel so much. I haven't left the city in a long time." She rolled her eyes. "Anyway, Lukasz's stall is just off the square, on the other side. You'll see the purple awning. Step through, follow the alley back, and—well, it's a bit complicated if you're not familiar with the streets, I guess. Why don't I take you there? I'm not busy."

"That's so kind, thank you!" Cordalles reached out her hand, and the girl shook it. "I'm Cordalles."

"I'm Raisha. Beautiful hawk, by the way." She looked longingly at Halawir. "I've always wanted a spirit animal. He *is* your spirit animal, I assume?"

"Yes," Cordalles answered. "But he's a—" She caught herself and stopped just in time. Halawir wondered what Raisha's reaction would be if she discovered he was a Great Beast. Cordalles laughed a little. "He's an odd one. Stubborn. We're still getting used to each other."

The girl laughed too, tossing her head back so that her hair rippled and shone in the sun. "Oh, they make it sound so easy, don't they? Summon a spirit animal, have a companion for life, have your skills and your senses elevated. But it's never that simple, of course." She started walking around the edge of the square and beckoned Cordalles to come with her. "It's just this way."

Cordalles followed Raisha a few steps behind and whispered into Halawir's feathers. "She's nice, isn't she, Halawir? That's why I always love docking. You get to talk to new people, not just the same boring mast-monkeys from the ship. And everyone's friendly, too. I've seen it in port towns in Eura, Zhong, Nilo. . . . Wherever you go, people love to chat to traders. They love hearing news from around the world." She sighed a little wistfully. "I don't understand why Mother and Father are always so scared for me." She took a few running steps forward to catch up with Raisha, so they wouldn't lose her in the crowded plaza.

For Raisha was small and quick. She seemed excited to have the chance to break out of her everyday routine and show a stranger around her city, and it put an added energy into her step.

Cordalles was usually just as nimble on the boat. But here on land, she seemed to Halawir like a fish out of water. Her usual sure step was more hesitant, as though her confidence was replaced with nerves—or maybe she just hadn't gotten her land legs yet.

Halawir felt for the girl, kept by her parents from learning to be comfortable mingling with new people, in new places.

He had never wanted to give in to the charged connection he felt between them, but just for a moment, he relented. He gave Cordalles a touch of his keen eyesight and quick reflexes, making it simple for her to dodge the crowds and easily follow in Raisha's footsteps.

After leaping over a stray bottle and sidestepping a man swinging a large barrel, Cordalles gave Halawir a sly smile. He could tell she realized what had happened, and was pleased.

Raisha led them across the plaza, past the purple awning, and around a few twisty streets. They turned a corner into a narrow alley, and Halawir saw that they'd reached a dead end. The alley was lined by the backs of buildings, with no vendors in sight. It ended in a low wall with a closed door in it.

"Is that his store?" Cordalles asked Raisha, slowing down as she approached the wooden door.

"Not exactly," answered a familiar voice.

They spun around.

Back at the other end of the street was a middle-aged man with light brown skin, a neatly sculpted beard, and a dark tunic. A man that Halawir recognized immediately.

Zerif.

Zerif should have felt like a friend, but everything in Halawir screamed at him to keep his distance. Because there was something strange about Zerif now, he realized. There was a spiral mark on his forehead. At first Halawir assumed it was a tattoo, but then the spiral pulsed under Zerif's skin.

Halawir shuddered, his skin prickling below his feathers.

What *was* that thing squirming on Zerif's brow?

"Halawir the Eagle. Great Beast and old friend, it's so good to see you again."

Cordalles turned to Halawir. "You know him?"

Halawir twitched his wings. It was hard, without words, to communicate that this man had been his ally in the war. This was the man that Halawir, Kovo, and Gerathon had helped to create the Bile. The man that Halawir had conspired with to release Kovo from prison.

"Oh, Halawir and I have known each other for quite some time," said Zerif. "We've always been a terrific team. In fact, that's why I was so pleased to find you two here today. I'm hoping to team up with him again. I know you won't mind."

Zerif pulled a black glass vial out from the pocket of his tunic. It caught the slanted rays of sunlight and fractured them into glittering rainbows. Halawir's sharp eyes allowed him to see clearly through the bottle's tinted glass, though—and what he saw gave him chills.

Inside the vial was a slithering dark shape, like the trail of a slug or a clot of grease suspended in dirty water. It twisted and writhed and shivered. It was just a shadow behind the dark glass, but enough to cause Halawir's stomach to turn with an unaccustomed emotion: fear. The thing was a creature, a worm, a smudge of moldy evil. It made Halawir think of foul smoke in a clear sky.

"Hold her," Zerif commanded.

Raisha darted over to Cordalles, grabbed her arms, and pinned them behind her back.

"What are you doing?" Cordalles screamed.

As Raisha had grabbed Cordalles's arms, Halawir tumbled from his perch. With a few sweeps of his wings, he regained his balance and flew to the end of the leather tether, as far from Raisha as he could go.

What was Zerif's plan? Halawir hesitated, unsure if he should attack or wait. Was Zerif a friend or an enemy? Was he there to rescue Halawir from the girl and allow him to regain his freedom?

But Halawir's eye was caught again by the bulging spiral on Zerif's forehead. There was something more going on. He had a vague memory of Kovo rambling during his years of imprisonment, talking about some sort of evil associated with this symbol, but he had never taken the ape seriously. What was it he had said . . . ?

Zerif undid the clasp of his tunic, letting the cloth fall away from his torso. He was wearing nothing underneath, and his bare skin shone in the sun. He began to uncork the vial as he slowly approached Halawir.

Friend or foe? Zerif was a former ally, but this spiral whispered of some unknown danger.

Halawir's nerves sung out, and with his whole body he suddenly knew that Zerif was no longer to be trusted.

He tensed, prepared to peck Zerif's eyes out the second he took another step.

But at that moment Cordalles wrenched her torso out of Raisha's grasp and threw her arm out and up with all her force.

Halawir was catapulted into the sky. He was so accustomed to the leash at this point that he waited for the moment when he reached the end of the tether.

He waited.

And it never came.

Cordalles had let go of the jess as she hurled him away from her. Freeing him.

A moment passed before he realized that his body had understood this fact long before his mind did, and that his wings were beating hard. They were propelling him away from danger.

He was high in the sky, on a sweet current of spring breeze. Below him he could see the whole city spread out like a child's puzzle, and around it, a patchwork quilt of field and forest.

Halawir the Great Beast was free at last.

He cried out, exulting. Somewhere in that maze of buildings, he knew, were Zerif and Raisha—and Cordalles, caught in a tussle.

But he had been the one they wanted, not Cordalles. Surely, he reasoned, they would let her go, now that she no longer had the thing they desired. He flew higher and higher. This was best. Sever the bond. Save himself, and render her useless. Zerif and Raisha would let her run back to her parents and the boat, and she'd return to her life like it was before.

But something caught at him, somewhere between his tail and his beak.

He craned his neck to see what it was. There was nothing there. It was an invisible stone in his belly, sinking him back down toward the earth.

She had freed him.

Cordalles had let him go.

He was flying down now, back down away from the sun and the clouds and freedom. He circled in on the city, the market, until he spotted the three tiny figures making their way out of the alley.

Zerif was walking ahead. Halawir could see by his stride that he was furious.

Behind him, Raisha led a struggling Cordalles. Her wrists were bound behind her. She pulled and resisted, trying to break free. Raisha yanked her roughly, and Cordalles tripped and fell to her knees.

That was it. He wouldn't stand for this.

Halawir dove. He plummeted from the sky like a falling star, heading straight at Raisha. He grabbed her long hair in his talons, startling her, and pulled with all his might.

"Agh!" she shrieked, stumbling backward. "Let go! Let go!" She brought her free hand up to try to yank Halawir away, and he tore mercilessly into her hand with his beak, drawing blood.

It worked. Raisha screamed and doubled over, her hand clutched to her chest, releasing Cordalles.

Cordalles immediately took off at a sprint, and Halawir gave her every last ounce of agility and fleetness that he could.

Zerif lunged at her. She darted out of his grasp and zigzagged down the alley, Zerif close on her heels, but Cordalles had a head start and the speed of an eagle driving her forward.

Halawir stayed behind. He pulled on Raisha's hair again, dragging her back. He could hear as strands ripped from her head, but mercy was not a thing that Halawir often found in his heart. He yanked again, only half his attention on the struggling girl. He was watching Cordalles run: As soon as Cordalles got far enough away, Halawir would release Raisha and make his own escape.

But suddenly he realized Zerif was no longer chasing Cordalles.

Where was he?

Halawir saw the movement a moment too late.

Zerif was next to them, and he sprang forward and wrapped his thick arm around Halawir's wings, pinning them to his sides.

With his free hand, he still held the vial.

"Quit your crying," he hissed at Raisha, who was screaming and grabbing at her hair. She quieted. Halawir tightened his feet in her hair even more, scratching her skull. She whimpered, but bit down on her lip to keep from crying out again.

Halawir was trapped. But at least the two of them were occupied, giving Cordalles a chance to get away. He hoped she kept running as fast and as long as she could, straight to the boat, never looking back.

"Hold still now," Zerif muttered. "First you must submit, but soon you'll have some of that power you love so very much."

He tipped the vial over, dropping the wriggling worm onto Halawir's chest. The parasite squirmed underneath Halawir's tawny feathers. He tried to crane his neck down to peck the thing out, but it moved too quickly. Once it reached his skin, it bit into him. Then it was under his skin. It wriggled and squirmed. He could feel it writhing its way up toward his head.

Halawir let out a tremendous cry.

Zerif dropped him at last. Freedom! Halawir let go of his grip on Raisha and spread his wings to take off.

But then he felt the thing curl up inside his forehead. All of the fight seeped out of him. He no longer felt his fierce fighting spirit. He relaxed his wings.

Footsteps pounded at the edges of his attention.

"Halawir!"

It was Cordalles. Running back for him once she heard his cry. He wanted to go to her, but a strange fog was drifting into his mind. He sank down and folded his wings onto his back as whispering voices drowned out his own instincts. He calmly sat and watched as Zerif grabbed Cordalles by the neck. He took another dark vial out from his tunic—only to have it knocked out of his hand.

"Let her go, Zerif."

In a small, shadowed corner of his mind, Halawir noted that a figure in a crimson cloak and an odd white mask had appeared and was trying to get between Zerif and Cordalles.

Or was he hallucinating? The red cloak and the black tunic swirled together like nightmare fireworks.

Who was the masked figure? Was he going to save Cordalles?

Halawir would never know. The last thing he saw before the fog overcame him was Raisha giving the masked man a shove, and the look of horror on Cordalles's face as Zerif closed in.

RUMFUSS

THE TRUNSWICK BLADE

By Nick Eliopulos

DEVIN TRUNSWICK WAS RUNNING OUT OF THINGS to sell.

He'd sold his jacket to a traveling merchant outside Trynsfield. It had been a fine jacket once, with polished buttons and a neat velvet trim. After months on the road, however, it had become tattered and travel stained. When Devin finally sold it, he barely got enough coin for a week's worth of food.

He'd sold his belt buckle to a shopkeeper in Samis. A gleaming silver rectangle engraved with the image of a sleek panther, it had been a gift from his father and, briefly, his most prized possession. Eventually, it served only to remind him of his failures. He couldn't bear to look at it, and so he sold it for a fraction of its worth.

The coin from that sale hadn't lasted him long. Devin had never been very good with money. He'd never had to worry about it before.

Lately it was near the top of a long list of worries.

"You're charging *how much*?" he said now, fuming, as he stood in the common room of a roadside inn.

"You heard me," the innkeeper responded, not bothering to look up as he wiped a dirty counter with a dirty rag. "So then, do you want a room or not?"

The man gazed meaningfully out the open doorway, where rain came down in heavy sheets. Devin had made it indoors just before the downpour started. He had hardly believed his luck, to have stumbled upon shelter just as the storm descended.

Now his luck appeared to be returning to form.

"Listen," Devin said through a clenched jaw. "I'm not some simpleminded rube with a head full of rotten teeth. I know what a cot and a meal is worth." He cast a scornful glance about the dimly lit room. A few scattered customers sat about, staring into their mugs or the fire and pretending not to notice the argument.

"It's my inn," the innkeeper said sourly. "A bed here's worth precisely what I charge and no less, boy."

Devin huffed. "I'm no *boy*."

The innkeeper's eyes roamed down Devin and up again, taking in his threadbare traveling cloak, filthy hands, and worn-out boots. "I know exactly what you are," the man snarled. "You're just another worthless urchin bothering the decent and hardworking folk of Eura. Well, you'll get no charity from me . . . *boy*."

Heat rushed to Devin's cheeks and a sharp retort leaped to his tongue, but he swallowed it back. "I'm not asking for charity," he said after a moment. He pulled a ring from his finger. It was only pewter—he'd long ago sold his more valuable jewelry—but it was fashionable and well made, shaped liked a circle of interlocking tree branches.

He slapped it onto the bar. "Surely that's worth a cot for the night and provisions for the road, too."

The innkeeper barely looked at it. "I don't barter," he said. "Coin only." Then he rubbed his chin thoughtfully. "I might barter for the sword."

Devin stiffened. "My sword?"

"Aye."

There was a moment of silence as Devin seemed to consider it. Then he said, "You have a fine eye, friend innkeeper." He spoke the words smoothly, but his eyes had gone fierce. "This sword is the workmanship of the finest craftsman in Eura—the queen's own blacksmith." He caressed the sword's hilt, the only part of the weapon visible while it was sheathed at his hip. "The hilt is grooved for comfort and ease of use. You could swing it three hundred times and never get a blister." He pulled the sword partway out of the scabbard, and a high metal sound rang out. "The steel is flawless, forged from Trunswick iron with charcoal made from Trunswick timber. The blade is perfectly balanced and sharp enough to cut bone." He slammed the weapon back into its scabbard and jabbed his finger in the innkeeper's face. "You aren't fit to touch this sword," he snarled. "It is worth more than this entire filthy, damp, lice-ridden hovel."

The innkeeper didn't flinch away from Devin's finger or from the spittle that flew from Devin's mouth.

"Brutis," he said calmly. "See the boy out, would you?"

A chair scraped heavily against the wood floor, and Devin turned to see the man by the fire lumber to his feet. Brutis was huge, easily four hands taller than Devin, and his arms were thick with muscle.

"Er," Devin said to the innkeeper, dropping his finger. "Perhaps we could start over?"

But the innkeeper had resumed running his dirty rag over the dirty countertop, and he didn't even bother to look up as Devin was dragged away and hurled outside, landing on his back in the mud with an audible plop.

Devin had always had a problem with his temper. He was trying to be better about it. He had a new trick: Every time he felt his cheeks grow hot, he would clamp his jaw shut and count slowly to ten before saying or doing anything.

That was the idea, anyway. But his mouth tended to be just a little faster than his brain.

The rain had stopped after only a quarter hour, but in that time he'd been thoroughly soaked. On the bright side, the water had been pleasantly warm. Devin couldn't remember the last time he'd had a proper bath, and he took the opportunity to rub at his hands and face, rinsing the dirt away.

In the aftermath of the rain, however, Devin knew true misery. His traveling cloak was sopping, and it hung heavily from his shoulders, a dead weight that kept his back from drying. His boots squelched with each step, and he could feel new blisters forming atop the old. His clothing clung to him, chafing in places he'd rather not chafe, and altogether his gear felt twenty pounds heavier than it had when dry.

Still, he trudged on, walking through the storm and through the muck and gnats and mugginess that came in its wake. He walked through the headache brought on by the shrill cry of a bird of prey, circling high above; he walked until the sun set and night descended and he was too tired to continue. Then he set up camp among the trees, just off the road.

He started a small fire, hung his cloak from a low branch to dry, and took stock of his meager possessions. It would be boiled oats for dinner. Again.

While he waited for water to boil in his battered tin pot, he sat upon a fallen trunk and stretched his legs. The only sounds were the crackling of the fire . . . and the rustling of an animal approaching through the fallen leaves.

Devin remained seated but twisted a bit to get a look at the woods around him. He was in the middle of a heavily forested area—acre upon acre of trees, with a single dirt road leading through it.

He'd finally crossed into Trunswick land earlier that day. Everything he could see, everything for miles around, belonged to his father.

Except perhaps for the fiercely independent creature watching him from the shadows.

"I see you," Devin said, addressing the glowing yellow eyes. "Come on out. It's almost time for dinner."

But the cat would not be hurried.

Eventually, at her own leisurely pace, a small black cat slinked from the trees and into the light of the fire. For a moment, he was reminded of his spirit animal, Elda, but he forced the thought away. Like so many others, Devin had lost his spirit animal bond in the aftermath of the war.

The cat meowed plaintively, sitting in the dirt a few paces away.

"Yeah, yeah," he said. "I'm working on it. Are all Greencloaks so impatient?"

The cat meowed again in response to Devin's favorite joke. When he'd first seen her, she had been traveling with a group of Greencloaks. But they had moved on, and the cat had struck out on her own . . . though she had a tendency to pop up each night when Devin was cooking.

He'd heard them call her Kunaya, but he called her Yaya for short.

"Careful, now," he said as he poured a small bit of oatmeal onto the ground for her. "It's hot."

Kunaya, as always, appeared initially wary, stepping forward slowly, sniffing as she walked. Eventually she decided the risk was worth the reward and darted forward, tucking happily into the boiled oats.

"It's a rare man who earns the trust of a cat," said an unfamiliar voice.

Devin stood, turning toward the sound as Kunaya bolted in the other direction, her meal unfinished. He put his hand to his sword but didn't draw it as a girl stepped out from the trees, leading a horse by the reins. She looked a little younger than him, but her bearing was confident, and she spoke with the poise of the educated upper class. "Cats are awfully particular about who they cozy up to."

"Maybe," Devin said, eyeing the girl warily. "Or maybe they just have keen noses and follow the food."

She shrugged. "Maybe a little of both. But I'm sore from riding and your fire looks inviting, so I'm going to assume that your willingness to share food with an animal is a sign that you're trustworthy. Now, is there room at your fireside for a fellow traveler?" When Devin took a moment to consider it, she added, "I have bacon to contribute."

Devin's mouth watered at the mere mention of bacon, but he tried not to let his excitement show. He simply nodded and gestured for the girl to pull up a log. "I suppose the cat would like that," he said.

The girl tied her horse to a tree and plopped down, grunting at the ache in her muscles. Devin tucked his chin down to hide his smile but kept his eyes on her. Her long hair was newly tangled, but it was a healthy, glossy black. She smelled of an odd mix of perfume and horse, and her riding clothes were a little too fashionable to be comfortable.

"What's so funny?" the girl asked.

"Nothing," Devin said. "You just remind me of myself. First time on the road?"

She gave him a suspicious look as she pulled a sheet of oiled parchment from her satchel, unrolling it to reveal several thick cuts of raw bacon. "I've traveled a lot," she said, a little defensively. She handed him two strips, which he placed on the pan. When they began to sizzle, she turned her eyes back to Devin. "But I've never gone quite so far by myself. How much farther to Trunswick?"

"You're on Trunswick land already," Devin answered. "If you ride at a fair clip, you could reach town in a few hours."

"That's a relief," she said. "I'd hate to miss the celebration."

Devin gave her a confused look. "Celebration?"

She smiled like a child with a secret. "Haven't you heard? It's all anyone's talking about."

"I've been keeping to myself recently," Devin said, and he flipped the bacon with a stick.

"Well, it's big news," she said. "Apparently the Earl of Trunswick's son has summoned a spirit animal. And not just any spirit animal—"

"Really?" Devin interrupted, his cheeks growing hot. "That's big news? You're months behind. Everyone knows Devin Trunswick summoned a black wildcat."

"I know *that's* old news," the girl said smugly. "I'm talking about the *other* Trunswick boy."

Devin sat in stunned silence for a long moment. He could scarcely make sense of the girl's words.

"Dawson?" he said at last, his voice small. "Dawson summoned a spirit animal?"

"Dawson Trunswick, that's right. And there's more," she said. "He summoned a Great Beast."

"Just like . . . just like Conor," Devin muttered to himself. "Of course. Of course it would happen like that." His stomach twisted. "Fa–the Earl of Trunswick must be so pleased."

"By all accounts, yes," the girl replied, giving a leisurely shrug. "The way I hear it, the earl's popularity suffered during the war. When the Greencloaks came to Trunswick, many of the townsfolk sided with them. Tensions have been high ever since–but with a Great Beast in the family, the Trunswicks have the respect of the people again. Talk of rebellion is dying out. Ah, the bacon . . . ?"

Devin turned to see the bacon was beginning to char. Acrid smoke hovered low in the pan. "Curse it," he said, grabbing the handle.

"It's no reason to get upset," she said. "I like it crispy. Anyway, the earl is having a celebration for his son. Everyone who's anyone will be there . . . provided you bring a grand enough gift to honor Dawson. My father sent me with enough spices to make my horse walk lopsided."

She lapsed into silence as Devin served up the bacon. It was thoroughly ruined, bitter and brittle on his tongue, but Devin ate it slowly, grinding it to gristle and ash in his teeth.

The silence was broken by the shrill cry of a bird. It sounded to Devin's ears like the same hawk or eagle he had heard throughout the day, but he knew those birds were not active at night.

The girl seemed startled by the sound. "I'd better be on my way," she said lightly as she got to her feet. "Big day tomorrow. I can't believe I'm meeting Dawson Trunswick!"

"Yeah, how about that," Devin said sourly.

"Thanks for the hospitality," she said. "I'm Raisha, by the way. See you around?"

She gave a small curtsy and was gone.

Devin tried to put Dawson out of his mind during the long day that followed. The thought of his brother with a spirit animal, however, was like a loose tooth he couldn't stop wiggling. It was easy to picture Dawson enjoying the status and adoration that having a spirit animal would bring—easy because Devin had imagined that life for himself for so long.

But things hadn't worked out that way.

Making his mood fouler was the fact that traffic on the dirt road he traveled was unusually heavy. Before the sun had even climbed above the trees, Devin was overtaken by four separate horse-drawn carriages, all headed in the direction of town. The dirt road was narrow enough that he was forced to step into the brush each time to avoid getting run over. Most of the carriages didn't seem to care whether or not he was trampled; they didn't slow down, and made no real effort to make room for him.

Each time he was forced off the path, he bit his tongue and counted to ten in his head.

As Devin walked, the road widened and the trees grew less dense, the forest giving way first to rolling hills and then to the great expanse of farmland that surrounded the town for miles on all sides. But there were no shepherds tending their flocks and no farm-hands working those lands. The entire countryside was empty. Devin was certain the people had set their work aside to visit Trunswick, as they did for holidays, market days, and Nectar Ceremonies.

He tried to forget about the humiliation of his own ceremony, but it hung around him like the cloud of midges he had been swatting at for the better part of the day.

And the memories came flooding back to him as he entered the town and found its dirt roads crowded to capacity and beyond. He smiled smugly as he passed the same carriages that had overtaken him hours before. They stood still now, a long line of them unable to make their way through the teeming crowds.

It was an oddly subdued affair. There were market stalls and musicians, but no dancing. The traders kept their voices low rather than crowing about their bar-gains, and soldiers wearing the traditional Trunswick blue glared from open doorways.

No one spared him a glance as he made his way through the crowd. He fit in all too well. In a perfect world, he mused, he would have been able to bathe before approaching his family's manor. He would have been able to trade his travel-stained clothes for finery, and run a comb through his tangled brown hair.

But he had not lived in a perfect world for some time.

As if to underscore the point, Devin noticed something then that made him deeply uneasy. At the very center of town, upon the stage where he had once drunk the Nectar to no effect, a woman was being tortured.

She was hunched over at an awkward angle, her head and hands locked between wooden boards, her bare feet chained to the stage. Devin had heard this form of punishment referred to as "the stocks." It was deeply uncomfortable, used to punish and publicly shame criminals, sometimes for many days and nights in a row. The woman's face was pink from exposure to the sun, and her lips were dry and cracked. But her eyes were defiant, as if daring the crowd to jeer.

No one did. Aside from the guard standing beside her, the people of Trunswick gave the stage a wide berth.

Devin picked up his pace.

The closer he got to the manor, the richer the crowd appeared. Those clustered about the manor's gates were all smartly dressed, their arms laden with gifts as they awaited entry.

Devin walked right up to the guard at the gate. Instead of wielding a sword or pike, the man held a quill poised above a vellum scroll.

"Please declare your gift," the guard said without looking up.

Devin grinned. "Oh, I promise Dawson will be happy with my *presence*." He chortled at his own joke.

"I haven't heard that joke in five whole minutes," the guard groused. "There's no admittance to the grounds without acceptable tribute."

Devin huffed imperiously. "I live here, you oaf."

The guard startled, finally looking up from his scroll. "Devin Trunswick?" he asked, uncertain.

Devin smiled and puffed out his chest. "Good. I'd hate to think a few months away and a bit of road dust was enough to be forgotten."

"Oh, I remember you," the guard said acidly. "You're the one who put a spiked caltrop in my chair."

Devin deflated a bit. "I'm almost certain that was Dawson," he lied.

"I have my orders," the guard said. Then he softened. "The earl, he . . . left very specific instructions about who to let in today. For what it's worth, I'm sorry."

"For what it's worth," Devin said, "I'm sorry, too."

Then he kicked him in the shin, hard. The guard toppled to the ground, and before any of the onlookers could react, Devin had ducked through the gate and onto the manor grounds.

There was a smaller group gathered in the courtyard, all lavishly dressed in the latest fashions. With no hope of blending in, he wove and dodged among them, ignoring their exclamations of surprise and distaste. He stepped on the trail of one woman's gown and nearly knocked a glass from a man's grip. Finally he made it into the manor itself, where the grand hall was empty.

The ceiling arched high above him in a perfect dome, layered in vibrant shades of blue and pink and orange in an uncanny approximation of the sky at dawn. The painted clouds were brilliant white at their center but ringed in shining gold leaf, and the hundred lit candles set about the hundred ledges and crevices of the circular room made the colors flicker as if alive.

He had seen this room every day for years. But today, for the first time, it took his breath away.

"Let me guess," said a voice behind him. "It's smaller than you remembered, right? That's what they always say. . . ."

Devin turned to see Dawson standing in the doorway. His brother's expression was blank, and he had his arms crossed in front of him as he lingered on the threshold.

"Well, they're wrong," Devin said. "It's so big. I . . . I don't think I had any idea how *rich* we are."

Dawson clucked his tongue. "And you traded all of this for a life of adventure?" he said. Then his face lit up with his familiar smile—big and goofy and unselfconscious. "You had the right idea. Take me with you!"

Devin laughed and opened his arms, and his little brother crossed the room quickly and embraced him.

"I was worried about you," Dawson said when they pulled apart.

Devin swatted at the air. "Nothing to worry about. I can take care of myself. Didn't you get my letters?"

"Letters?" Dawson asked, and before Devin could answer, he felt the hair on the back of his neck stand on end and a shiver down his spine.

He had always had an uncanny ability to sense when their father was nearby.

"Devin!" The earl barked the name, short and sharp. It sounded like a curse.

Devin turned to face his father, who stepped into the room with an armed guard at each elbow. They moved briskly, stirring up a breeze that extinguished the nearest candles, shrouding them in shadow.

"You've always been thick, boy, but really, take a hint."

"Father . . ." Devin said, and the earl's eyes flashed with anger.

"*You*," he seethed, "will address me as Lord Trunswick. On your way out the door."

Devin felt the words like a blow to the stomach. He didn't know what to say, how to react, or even where to look. So he looked at the ground.

"That's uncalled for, Father," Dawson said. He gripped Devin by the elbow. "It's my party. I want Devin here for it."

Devin looked up at his brother—and realized that Dawson was taller than him now. He marveled at the resolve in Dawson's eyes as he stared down their father.

When had Dawson grown so bold?

"At least tell me you've brought Dawson some gift as tribute," the earl said to Devin. He gestured to a table weighed down with everything from bolts of silk and jewels to vials of exotic spices.

Devin tried to mimic the resolve in Dawson's expression. "I don't have anything," he said, careful to keep his voice level. "When I didn't hear from you, I had to sell everything I had just to get back here."

His father sniffed imperiously. "The sword should do nicely, I think."

Devin bristled. "It's my sword."

"It's the *Trunswick* sword," the earl countered. "It's only fitting–"

Devin drew the blade then, and the shrill sound of metal rang out like a threat.

"I'm not sure you'll be happy with it, *Lord Trunswick*," Devin said. "Since it's not perfect."

He held up the blade so that it caught the light of the candles. It was broken to half its original length, ending in an ugly jagged edge.

"Unbelievable." His father glared at him. "Tell me, did you accomplish *anything* in your time as a Conqueror?" He covered his eyes with his hand. "Do you realize we had to abduct some ridiculous sheep woman and hold her hostage because you couldn't get your hands on a single talisman? You ruined this family, Devin."

"That's enough!" Dawson cried. He stepped between them, threw back his shoulders, and held out his arm dramatically. There was a flash of light . . . and Devin saw a squat, bristle-haired animal snorting and wheezing at his brother's feet.

It was Rumfuss the Boar.

Devin laughed, deep and loud.

"Rumfuss? You summoned Rumfuss?"

Uncertainty flickered across Dawson's face. "What's so funny?"

Devin cleared his throat. "Nothing, nothing. Don't mind me. It's just that when I heard you'd summoned a

Great Beast, I'd imagined something a bit more . . . majestic. Not . . . you know . . ."

Rumfuss and Dawson both huffed in agitation.

"Rumfuss is a Great Beast," Dawson said. "He is powerful and . . . and . . ."

"And put an apple in his mouth and dinner is served!" Devin said. "You know what the Conquerors used to call Rumfuss? The great bore." He cackled. "Get it? *Bore?*"

The spirit animal let out a deep rumbling growl—and then he charged.

Rumfuss had once been much larger. Like the other reborn Great Beasts, his new form was much closer to the size of a natural animal, and so he was only slightly larger than an average boar.

But an average boar is thickly built and vicious, with razor-sharp tusks capable of gutting a person in a single glancing blow.

Devin knew this. And seeing the two-hundred-pound animal bearing down on him, he shrieked, leaping back and bringing his hands up to protect his body. For all the good that would do. Those tusks would cut right through his fingers. . . .

It was a long several moments before Devin realized the boar was gone. He lowered his hands and opened his eyes, which he had squeezed shut, and confirmed it: His brother had recalled his spirit animal and now stood before him, his fists clenched and his eyes furious.

"You were right, Father," Dawson said coldly. "I think it's best if Devin left now."

"Now hold on," Devin said. "I'm sorry, I didn't—"

"Guards!" the earl barked. "Do as my son says." He leveled his steely gaze at Devin. "And throw this useless fool out on his ear."

Devin knew he'd messed up.

It was a familiar feeling, but no more comfortable for that fact. It always happened the same way—he got angry, and then he got mean. And then when the anger eventually faded, he found himself regretting what he'd said and done.

He'd found an inn that was crowded enough to allow him to blend in, but empty enough that he could have a table to himself. He sat alone, nursing a mug of chocolate he'd bought with one of his few remaining coins, and he wondered where he should go now.

He couldn't stay in Trunswick. With dark humor he realized he couldn't afford the earl's taxes.

As Devin gazed out the window onto the darkening street, he saw a familiar face—one he would never have expected to see here. He scrambled up from the table and ran outside as the cloaked figure turned a corner at the end of the street.

The crowds were just as thick as they'd been during the day, slowing Devin down. By the time he made it to the corner, all he found was an empty alleyway.

He cursed. Then he turned around, and Karmo was standing there, blocking Devin's exit from the alleyway.

Devin and Karmo had been partners during the war.

They had both been recruited by a man named Zerif, a high-ranking Conqueror with a vicious streak. But they'd failed on their first mission, and Zerif had abandoned them, leaving them imprisoned in a castle to the north.

"Karmo." Devin smiled. "I'm so glad to see you."

"I was just thinking the same thing," Karmo said—and then he attacked.

Karmo launched himself at Devin. The Niloan boy got in a punch—a solid right hook to the temple—before Devin could even get his hands up.

Devin's head snapped back, but he rolled with the blow, twisting around and grabbing Karmo's wrists in an iron grip.

Karmo was fast, but Devin was bigger and stronger. He squeezed.

Then he felt a sudden tingling pain in his palms, as if he'd been shocked. He pulled his hands back, and Karmo took the opportunity to land a head butt.

Devin saw stars. He brought his hands up to his aching face. "Just . . . just hold on," he said.

"That isn't half of what you've got coming," Karmo said.

"Really?" Devin asked. "I thought we left on good terms. . . ."

"*You* left!" Karmo countered. "You left me in prison, you idiot!"

"My dad bailed me out," Devin said. "And threw me right back into the war. Honestly, even if I could have brought you with me, I figured you were better off."

Karmo glared at him.

"As prisons go, it wasn't that bad," Devin insisted.

"I had to listen to MacDonnell coo at his rabbit for months, Devin. He made his musicians compose a heroic ballad about that rabbit, and he'd sing it wherever he went. It's been stuck in my head for months. . . ." Karmo shuddered.

"I'm sorry," Devin said.

Karmo seemed surprised by that. "You're sorry?"

"Yeah."

Karmo thought about it. He shrugged. "Okay." He paused. "I'm sorry I hit you. I was angry."

"You should try counting to ten," Devin offered. He rubbed his aching face. "What are you even doing here?"

"You're not going to like it," Karmo admitted with a sigh. He leaned against the alley wall. "I'm here for Dawson. Zerif's hunting Great Beasts. He's found some way to . . . to steal spirit animals. Not just carry away, but sever the bond completely."

Devin's blood went cold. "Is he here? Now?"

"I don't know." Karmo slapped the wall. "But your father may as well have sent an invitation with as much noise as he's been making about Dawson's summoning. I'm working with . . . someone who has a bit of a grudge against Zerif. And since you and I have history, I thought I had the best chance of warning your father. He laughed in my face and threw me out." He smiled. "But hey! Now you're here. You can get a warning to your brother. Better yet, get him out of town. I can take him someplace safe."

"That . . . might be a problem. I'm not exactly welcome back home."

Karmo sighed dramatically. "Great. Of course. I'm no better off than I was before you showed up."

"Not true," Devin said. "I can get to Dawson. I just need to get past my father's guards."

Karmo shook his head. "From what I've seen, they're loyal to him. And that's lucky for him, because the rest of the town hates his guts."

"Really?"

"Oh, yeah," Karmo said. "I've been here for two days, and I've overheard a lot. You know the woman in the stocks? She's there for suggesting your father should be put on trial for war crimes. She's not the only one who thinks so, but she said it the loudest."

"I didn't realize," Devin said softly. "I thought Dawson summoning a Great Beast had brought everyone together."

Karmo scoffed. "Your dad would like to think so. But the hurt runs too deep. He openly supported an invading army and imprisoned anyone who spoke out against it. Now he's pretending like it never happened—but he's nervous, so he brought on dozens of former Conquerors to beef up his personal guard. People have tried withholding taxes in protest, but he just sends the guards around to threaten them, which makes more people withhold taxes. . . ."

"My father is a bully," Devin said, realizing the truth as he voiced it. How had he never thought of it in those terms before?

After all, Devin had been called a bully his entire life. And he wasn't proud to admit it, but it had often been true. He'd pushed other kids around, teased them, threatened them.

No wonder. He'd learned that behavior from his father. But the Earl of Trunswick was bullying hundreds of people all at once.

"I think I've got an idea for how we can get to Dawson," Devin said.

"You *think*?"

"Well, I definitely have an idea." Devin rubbed his chin. "I'm just not sure if it's a good one or not."

"It's a bad plan," Karmo said as they walked together through the crowd. "A very bad plan."

"Maybe," Devin said. "But I know a thing or two about anger, and I think it'll work."

"Devin." Karmo gripped his shoulder. "Think it through, man. Once you push this boulder, it is rolling all the way downhill. I can try to tilt it one way or the other, but we won't be able to stop it again if you change your mind."

"As long as the Earl of Trunswick is in that boulder's path, I don't care."

Karmo bit his lip, searching Devin's face as if for any sign of hesitation. Finding none, he shrugged. "Whatever you say. I'll be ready to move."

Devin nodded and made his way to the wooden platform he'd seen earlier in the day. The same woman was still in the stocks. She had a faraway look in her eyes and didn't even seem to notice when Devin clambered his way onto the platform.

The guard noticed, however. He stepped forward immediately, raising his pike as if to ward Devin off.

"Stand down," Devin said, and though he looked nothing like a noble, he sounded the part. "I'm here on behalf of my father, the earl."

The guard looked uncertain, but nodded and took a step back.

Devin stepped to the woman. He held a waterskin to her lips and allowed her to drink her fill.

"I'm going to get you out of there," Devin whispered as she drank. "Hold on for just another few minutes."

The woman nodded as best she could, eyes sharp again, refreshed by the water.

He stepped to the front of the stage.

"People of Trunswick!" he called out, and whatever eyes weren't already on him turned his way almost immediately. "My name is Devin. I'm the firstborn son of the earl, and I'm here on behalf of my father to welcome you in this time of celebration."

The crowd clapped politely, and Devin paused for a moment before continuing.

"He'd come here himself, but he hates to get mud on his shoes." Devin forced a chuckle, and there was an awkward echo of forced chuckles scattered throughout the crowd. "There certainly is a lot of mud down here, isn't there?" he said to the guard, loud enough for everyone to hear.

"Anyway," he continued. "My father is a great and generous man. On the occasion of my own bonding, he gifted me with a gleaming belt buckle of purest silver. It was worth enough to feed a family for a month. I felt so grateful to him, knowing how many people were out there in the world starving while I wore silver around my waist.

"He liked to joke that his mastiffs ate better than the townsfolk.

"But his generosity doesn't extend just to his family. No indeed. Did you know that he's found work for the Conquerors? That's right. They lost the war, but the earl has seen fit to hire dozens of them to act as his personal guard. Didn't you notice how many soldiers have been in town lately? Didn't you notice how they look at Eurans with disdain? It's nothing personal. It's just that they were our enemies in a war until recently. I'm sure they don't hold any grudges, though."

Devin heard gasps from the crowd as he spoke, and could practically feel the heat as their gazes turned fiery. Still he pressed on.

"It's important to let grudges go if we're to heal in the aftermath of the war," Devin said. "I saw firsthand how my father was forced to lock up the people who disagreed with him when he first brought the Conquerors to Trunswick. I'm sure it was very upsetting for those of you who were temporarily jailed—or those whose loved ones were. But in hindsight, I think we can all agree that my father did the right thing and prevented anyone from getting hurt for what they believed in."

Devin grinned his most annoying grin. His father

had once threatened to lock him in the Howling House for smiling at him this way.

"My father's always done a good job of looking out for the people of this town. That's why he's raising taxes later this year—it's only at a great expense that he's able to keep you all safe by paying, housing, and feeding former Conquerors to act as his own personal peace-keeping force.

"In conclusion, I think we can all agree that my father is a great and generous man."

It worked almost too well.

Devin had whipped the crowd into a frothing, frenzied fury. Farmers had grabbed their pitchforks. Craftspeople had taken up torches. The guards who'd been left in town overnight were doing their best to contain the mob, but they were fighting a losing battle and they knew it.

By the time Devin was halfway up the hill to the manor, the guards had ignited a massive signal pyre in the town below—a sign that they needed reinforcements from the manor.

Devin slunk into the trees. It would slow his progress somewhat, but it would also keep him from being spotted by those reinforcements on their way into town. Soon he saw their torches on the other side of the trees, and he knew his plan had worked. The manor was unguarded, and Devin strolled right through the gate and into the front door as if he still belonged there.

He found his brother on the roof, sitting atop the sloping expanse of shingles just outside Dawson's bedroom window.

When they'd been little boys, they'd made a thorough search of the manor for secret, out-of-the-way places where they could hide from their father on days when his temper threatened to explode. He'd found them in the broom closets; he'd found them in the hedges. But given the earl's fear of heights, it never occurred to him to stick his head out a third-story window to look for them here. And even if he saw them, he'd never step onto the roof to come after them.

This hidden patch of roof had quickly become their favorite spot.

"You could have moved into my bedroom," Devin said as he clambered out Dawson's window. "It's bigger."

Dawson didn't look up or startle at his voice. He simply shook his head. "I wouldn't let anyone touch your room."

Devin smiled as he sat beside his brother. "You're standing up to him. Not letting him push you around." He put a hand on Dawson's shoulder. "I was worried, leaving you here with him. But you know how to handle him, don't you?"

Dawson didn't say anything. They sat together for a minute, sharing what Devin considered a comfortable silence.

Then he saw that his brother was silently crying.

"Hey, is this about what I said before? About

Rumfuss?" he asked. "I'm sorry, Dawson. I didn't mean it."

Dawson shook his head, wiped at his cheeks, sniffed. "It's not that. It's . . . After you left, Father and that horrible man with the beard—"

"Zerif," Devin clarified.

Dawson nodded. "They abducted Conor's mother. Held her prisoner. You heard him bragging about it." He took a shaky breath. "I helped them. I helped them take her, and then I went to Conor and told him that he had to hand over the talisman or . . . or else."

"That's not your fault," Devin said.

"Isn't it?" Dawson turned to look at him, and his eyes shone with new tears. "I could have refused. I could have saved her. Snuck her out. But I was too afraid."

Devin looked out over the dark manor grounds. He saw torches in the distance, moving up the hill from town. "I never should have left," Devin said.

Dawson sniffled. "It's okay, you—"

"Let me finish. I never should have left without you." Devin stood, balancing on the sloping rooftop.

"Careful," Dawson warned.

"Don't worry, I'm as nimble as a wildcat," Devin said. "But I can't stay here, Dawson. And I don't think you should stay here either."

You're in danger, he didn't say. But maybe he wouldn't have to. Maybe Dawson didn't need to know that he'd been targeted by Zerif.

His little brother looked up at him. "Are you serious?"

"Serious as an angry mob," Devin said, looking over his shoulder. "We need to leave tonight. Now. I have a friend who can help us get out of town."

A huge smile split Dawson's face. "You have a friend?"

"Yeah, well, he did punch me earlier, if that makes it easier to believe." Devin grinned. "Now pack your things. And, uh, maybe grab some jewelry, too. It turns out a life of adventure isn't cheap."

Devin left Dawson to pack. He had one more thing to take care of before he could leave, and he set his face in grim determination as he hurried down the hallway.

His grimness fell away, however, when he turned a corner and nearly collided with a familiar girl.

"Raisha?" he said, surprised. "What are—?" The girl was still dressed in her fine riding clothes, but she'd combed the tangles from her hair and washed the road dust from her face. Her tan skin and dark hair glowed warm and lovely in the torchlight.

A flicker of surprise lit her features, but it was fleeting, replaced with a playful roll of her eyes. "Thank goodness you're here. I'm so lost!" She placed a hand on his shoulder. "Where is the third-floor parlor room?"

"Uh, back there," Devin said, hooking a thumb over his shoulder. "Just past Dawson's room."

"Dawson's room." Raisha flashed her teeth in a wide smile. "Thanks."

Devin blinked after her as she continued up the hallway. He remembered she'd said she was coming with gifts from her merchant father. But why wasn't she more surprised to see him here? Had she actually known who he was all along?

He shoved the question aside. At the moment he decided he had more important things to dwell on.

He set his scowl back in place and walked downstairs to confront his father.

Devin found the earl in their opulent dining room. He was seated at the far end of a long table, which had been carved from a single massive oak and polished to a shine. There was room at the table for thirty. But tonight, his father dined with only a single guest.

It was Zerif.

"What's *he* doing here?"

"He was invited," the earl said, getting to his feet. "Unlike you."

Devin noticed his father's spirit animal curled up alone in the corner. The lynx's face was buried in its paws. He'd never seen it so sedate.

Zerif smiled languorously. His beard was as immaculate as ever, but there was a strange spiral of raised flesh upon his forehead, like a scar or a brand.

"Don't trust him." Devin gripped the hilt of his sword. "Father—Lord Trunswick—*please*. You have to listen. Zerif is targeting the Great Beasts. He's here for Dawson!"

Zerif laughed, deep and long. The sound set Devin's nerves on edge.

Devin drew his sword. The sound of ringing metal brought both men's eyes to the broken blade.

"Oh my, Lord Trunswick. Is that the family sword?" Zerif sneered at Devin's father. "You really have fallen on hard times, haven't you?"

The earl stiffened at the comment.

"Hard times?" Devin echoed.

He saw it then, and he felt like a fool for failing to see it before. He saw it in his father's rumpled suit with the unstarched collar. In the lynx's bowl, filled with oats instead of meat. He saw it in the absence of servants, and the almost desperate insistence on lavish gifts from foreign visitors.

"You're broke," Devin said. "Aren't you?"

His father shuffled across the room to pour himself a drink from a crystal decanter. He shrugged dramatically. "Wars are expensive. Particularly when you support the losing side."

"When you said I ruined the family . . ."

He scowled at Devin over the rim of his glass as he drank. "Did you think I was overstating things?" He wiped his mouth on his sleeve. "Thanks to you, I can tell you exactly how much a spirit animal costs. Or how much ransom MacDonnell charges for the release of a prisoner, however disgraced and useless that prisoner may be."

Zerif laced his fingers together. Devin found it deeply unsettling that the man was still sitting at the table, as calm as he'd ever seen him, utterly unbothered by Devin's drawn weapon. "Fortunately for your father,"

Zerif said, "I've been too busy to spend any of the coin he gave me for your little wildcat. And he has something of value left to sell."

The truth dawned slowly on Devin, because it was nearly unthinkable—and because he didn't want to believe it. But the guilt in his father's red-rimmed eyes confirmed it.

"I won't let you hurt Dawson," Devin said, and he raised his broken sword higher. "Neither of you."

"Not Dawson," his father said, and he sagged as if suddenly burdened with some tremendous weight. He moved to stroke his spirit animal, but the lynx hissed softly at his approach. His father sighed, retracting his hand. "They won't hurt Dawson. They just want the boar."

"They?" Devin said. And his eyes went from his father, to Zerif . . . to the third table setting, where the picked-clean bones of a small chicken sat upon a fine porcelain plate.

"Raisha," he whispered.

He turned and ran from the room, heedless of his father's cry for him to stop. He didn't even slow to sheathe his shattered sword but tore through the manor as fast as he could, cursing the size of the place as he crossed room after room, ascended two long flights of stairs, and navigated the top floor's twisty halls to at last arrive at Dawson's bedroom door. He rammed it open with his shoulder. The room was empty.

The slanting roof beyond the window was not.

"Well, look who figured it out," Raisha said as Devin clambered through the open window.

"Devin," Dawson said, almost sobbing in relief. He was backed up to the edge of the roof, and Raisha stood between him and the only accessible window. "She wants Rumfuss. She said if I don't summon him—"

"Don't," Devin said, keeping his eyes on Raisha. "Don't summon him. I'll get you out of his."

"Not with that sad excuse for a sword," Raisha said, and she raised her own dagger, a wicked, gleaming thing.

"It's not perfect," Devin said. "And it's lost a battle or two. But it's still sharp." He held it up. "What more do you need from a sword?"

He lunged, and Raisha knocked the blow aside.

She took a swing at him, but he leaned out of the path of her weapon.

They were well matched. For every strike, there was a parry. For every move, there was a counter. And all the while, they circled each other upon the roof, like dancers enraptured by a discordant song of clashing steel.

Devin had never won a fight. Not one-on-one like this.

But he didn't have to beat her. He only had to clear enough space for Dawson to escape.

Devin rode a surge of confidence. The strangeness he had felt since Elda's tattoo disappeared into his skin was working for him now. Maintaining his balance felt effortless, even on the sloping rooftop. His reactions were quick, and his eyesight was sharp in the darkness. He could see the beads of sweat forming on Raisha's brow.

"Dawson," he said. "Get ready."

But then he heard his brother shout a warning. An eagle shrieked, and talons raked across Devin's back.

He didn't fall. And he didn't drop his sword. He gritted his teeth against the pain, and he stood his ground.

But then Raisha kicked him in the stomach, and he crumpled. His sword clattered away across the tiles.

"Devin!" Dawson cried.

Zerif slinked through the open window. Devin tried to shout threats at the man, to warn him away from Dawson, but he couldn't catch his breath to speak. And anyway, Zerif didn't move toward Dawson. He stepped up to Devin, bending over to grab him by the throat.

"I want to clarify something," Zerif said lightly, and he lifted Devin up. Devin could barely breathe, and he clutched at Zerif's wrist. It wasn't until he heard Dawson cry his name again that he realized Zerif had positioned him over the side of the roof. His feet kicked empty air.

"When you bonded with that sad little wildcat," Zerif continued, "I told you that you were a more worthy hero than the Four Fallen." He smiled. "I lied. It's probably obvious to you by now that you're *not* worthy, but I wanted you to know that I knew that." He raised his voice. "Dawson! Introduce me to Rumfuss, or we'll see if your brother's skull is as thick as they say."

Devin took a choked breath through Zerif's crushing grip. "Don't do it, Dawson," he rasped. "Remember . . . remember that time I put tree sap in your hair?"

Zerif looked at him, amused.

"Remember," Devin said, "when I put all your clothing on the dogs, and set them loose in the mud?" He gasped another breath. "I want you to run, Dawson. Run and don't look back."

"I remember," Dawson said. "I remember every awful thing you ever did." Tears streaked his face, but his voice was steady. "I also remember other things. Like when I broke Father's favorite vase, and you took the blame because I was afraid. I love you, Devin."

Rumfuss appeared in a flash of light and stood motionless upon the roof. The boar's eyes found Devin's, and there was such sadness there that Devin could hardly bear to look.

"I'm sorry," he whispered to the boar.

With his free hand, Zerif hurled a small vial at Rumfuss. It broke on the Great Beast's tough hide, seemingly without causing harm. But after a tense few seconds, Rumfuss disappeared again. Dawson gasped as if in pain at the same moment Zerif let out a triumphant chortle . . . then released his grip on Devin.

He saw the look of surprise on Raisha's face, and the utter despair on Dawson's. And then he saw only the ground, three stories down and hurtling quickly upward to meet him.

If he'd had time to think about it, Devin would have been sure he was about to die.

But thinking had never been Devin's strong suit.

He acted on pure instinct, tucking his body and rolling through the air until he was falling belly first. Then he held out all four limbs, bent them just enough to make them limber—and he landed in the grass on his hands and feet.

The pain was sudden and intense, but that's how Devin knew he had survived.

And then he blacked out.

Devin awoke to the sight of two silhouetted figures looming above him. The light flickered dramatically, making it hard to focus, and for a moment he was afraid he'd damaged his vision.

But it was only fire. Fire was engulfing Trunswick Manor.

"Devin!" Dawson cried, and he embraced his brother. The talon marks on Devin's back flared in pain, but he didn't complain. He hugged his brother back.

"Man, that was impressive," Karmo said. "I saw you fall, and I thought, well . . . But you're like a cat." There was awe in his voice, but his eyes were suspicious, like he was seeing Devin in a whole new light.

But Devin was more concerned with Dawson, who appeared shaky and pale. He knew what a terrible feeling it was to lose a spirit animal bond. "We can still stop them," he said. "We can get Rumfuss back."

Dawson shook his head sadly. "They're long gone. And I . . . I can't feel Rumfuss anymore."

Devin winced. "I'm sorry, Dawson."

"Don't be sorry," Karmo said. "Be mad. Whatever Zerif is up to, he's just getting started. Come with me, and I can introduce you to some people who want him stopped." He looked over his shoulder. "Also, your house is on fire."

Devin could hear the shouts of the mob from around the front of the manor. They sounded like they were out for blood.

"I think Father is still inside," Dawson said. "Should we . . . ?"

"Let Lord Trunswick look after himself," Devin said. "It's what he does best."

Miles from the town, they could still see the blaze.

"Man, Devin," Karmo said, "you sure know how to burn a bridge."

"There's no going back," Dawson said. "Is there?"

Devin took a long last look at the great plume of smoke drifting lazily into the sky above the ruins of his childhood home. "I guess I'm hoping that where we're going is more important than where we came from."

"We'll get there," Dawson said. He was still pale, but he managed a smile. "Together."

"Together," Devin agreed. "And something tells me that we'll land on our feet."

SUKA AND
ARAX

A CHILL WIND

By Gavin Brown

FROM HER VANTAGE POINT HIGH ON A ROCKY CRAG, ANUQI watched the distant figure make its way across the glacier. The figure moved awkwardly, almost tripping with every step. It must be an outsider from the south, new to walking in snowshoes.

Strangers bring only broken promises and sorrow.

Those were the words her grandmother had always said whenever a visitor had come to Maliak. It was an old Ardu saying, passed down through the tribes of Arctica since the days when the first Euran traders had arrived. Bitter lessons of broken agreements and spoiled goods.

As a little girl, Anuqi hadn't believed her. She had loved the idea of mysterious strangers and longed to meet the Greencloaks who sometimes traveled her land. But since her grandmother had died during the Second Devourer War, those words had proven true over and over.

Anuqi glanced over at the nook where her spirit animal had once rested. The massive polar bear would sun herself while Anuqi stood sentry and searched the horizon for strangers.

She looked away, trying not to dwell on the loss. Grandmother had always believed in her. If Grandmother had been alive, she wouldn't have stood by and let her parents sell Anuqi's only friend.

It wasn't *just* strangers who gave sorrow and broken promises.

Ever since the Greencloaks had arrived and destroyed Suka's Ice Palace, the village of Maliak had posted a sentry on the mountainside. Strangers were no longer welcome here.

Today it was Anuqi's turn to climb to the point where the ice turned to rock and see if anyone was approaching.

Anuqi grimaced. She didn't want to go down and tell the village that there was a traveler arriving. Her turn as sentry was one of the few times she could be alone, far away from the traitors who called themselves her family.

She wasn't sure they deserved it. But if she didn't warn them, they would accuse her of doing a sloppy job and make her spend the days sharpening bone knives with her father instead of alone up here. She hopped up and started down, carefully stepping her way down the icy slope.

There had been a time when she could have bounded down the slope, drawing the strength and sure-footedness of Suka, her spirit animal and one of the reborn Great Beasts. But her bond with Suka was gone, and with it her fearlessness. Anuqi had only seen eleven winters, but these days it felt more like eighty.

After she had gotten back and let the village elders know that a visitor was approaching, Anuqi walked to her parents' tent. She walked more quickly as soon as she heard the yelping of the dogs. Why were they back? Her father should have been out with the fishing party, using his new sled to haul in their catch at the end of the day.

She'd barely had time to get inside, to take off her parka and breathe in the smothering smoky air, before her mother was in her face.

"What do you know about this? What haven't you told us?" her mother demanded. The short, stubby woman shoved a note in Anuqi's face.

Anuqi shrugged. She squinted at the piece of paper, but it was all squiggles to her. Some of the Arctican children in the larger settlements were learning to read, but Anuqi's family hadn't taken up the practice yet.

"I have no idea," she said, crossing her arms.

"If you've gone and brought more trouble on us . . ." Her mother's voice trailed off, but the glare that followed said enough.

"Calm down, Saniaka," her father said, placing a hand on his wife's shoulder. "She can't read. She doesn't even know what it says."

"I can read it for you, if you like," another man's voice said.

Anuqi looked beyond her parents to see a thin stranger sitting at the table. He was skinny, almost gaunt, and had the pale look of one of the Euran traders. Broken promises and sorrow, sitting right here in their tent, her grandmother would say.

"I was paid to find you and deliver this message, and I suppose that includes reading it if needed," he added.

Her mother glared at the man, but neither of her parents moved to stop him. He sighed, stood up, and took the paper in his hands.

"To Anuqi, spirit bond of the Great Beast Suka," the messenger read. "We can help restore what has been taken from you. Meet me at the last day of the waning moon, at the Smiling Fox Inn, in Radenbridge. Sincerely, A friend."

Anuqi gaped at the man. "Is this a joke? Is someone mocking me?" she demanded.

Her spirit animal, the Great Beast Suka, had been taken two months ago. Two strangers, a man and a girl, had arrived late one evening. Anuqi had seen them from her sentry post. That time Suka had been with her, the polar bear alternating between sunning herself on the rocks and wrapping around Anuqi, protecting her from the Arctican chill.

With Suka around, Anuqi had never been cold, and never lonely. Now both gnawed at her every day.

"What business does this 'friend' have demanding that Anuqi go all the way to Eura?" her mother asked.

"We can't afford the passage anyway," her father added. "The whole idea is laughable."

Anuqi eyed her parents. She didn't believe the message one bit, but it was exactly like them to not even consider what she thought. Just like last time.

The strangers had come straight to her tent and made an offer. The man with his trim beard and predatory scowl, and the girl with her smug air of superiority. Anuqi had mistrusted them immediately.

The man had made the village an offer: Let him take Suka, in exchange for a hefty bag of coins. Her parents had refused, of course. Suka was an ancient friend of the Ardu, her father had said. No amount of gold could buy their sacred bear.

Anuqi's mother had stalled the strangers while her father gathered a few friends from nearby. They arrived, armed with knives and clubs, and demanded that the strangers leave. Her father had looked like a hero, striding in with two other Ardu men to kick these frightening people out of their village.

Anuqi remembered pressing her head into Suka's fur, not wanting to see what happened next. She could hear the bear's angry growl as her spirit animal stared down the visitors. She expected to hear fighting, but instead there were bright flashes of light, and she was forced to look up.

The inside of the tent was suddenly a tumult. A massive boar appeared from thin air, followed by a ram and an eagle. Immediately the animals attacked the three men. Her father and his friends retreated, barely dodging tusks, horns, and talons.

Suka gave a great roar and charged at the bearded stranger, but the haughty girl jumped in from the side. Anuqi saw her slap something concealed within her hand—it looked like a small black vial—against the polar bear's head.

Suka suddenly stopped. The polar bear shook her head side to side in confusion, pawing at her own face. Then her eyes went wide and she lay down.

Anuqi remembered screaming. It had felt like her world was being torn apart, like every piece of her was twisting in a different direction. And then Suka had stood up, with a dead look in her eyes, and there was only icy emptiness inside Anuqi.

She had collapsed, shaking in pain and terror as her connection with Suka was shredded. The polar bear calmly padded over to stand next to the man and the girl. Anuqi's spirit animal and best friend in the world had left without even looking back.

"It seems the 'ancient friend of the Ardu' has made her own choice," the bearded man had said with a small smile. "Once again, she chooses freedom."

The last thing Anuqi had seen before blacking out from the pain was her mother accepting the bag of coins that the sneering girl offered her.

Her parents had tried to explain that they needed the money. That after the war and the poor hunting season, they barely had enough to feed themselves—let alone the sled dogs. Suka was gone anyway, her mother had said. But Anuqi hadn't spoken to her for weeks.

The pain had lessened as time passed, but it would never go away. It was as if she had been warming herself by a fire, only to have a snowdrift collapse onto it.

Anuqi put away thoughts of the past and glared at her parents. No, they didn't care what she felt or wanted. Not a bit.

"Your friend also sent this," the messenger said, handing Anuqi a small jingling pouch. It was heavy with coins. "Enough coppers to pay for the journey."

Anuqi grimaced. Another stranger with a bag of money—another disaster waiting to happen. Her parents just stared, her father in surprise and her mother in greed. Anuqi's grandmother hadn't cared for money, but since the Euran traders had started coming every year, all her mother could think of was how to earn enough to buy fancy goods and foreign spices.

"What is this?" her father demanded. "What are you playing at?"

"I'm sorry I can't offer more of an explanation. That's all I was told to do," the man said. "My duty is discharged. Now I have other deliveries to make. Farewell. And good luck, Anuqi."

Her mother hustled the man out the door. The moment the tent flap was shut, she snatched the bag from Anuqi's hands.

"Well, you're obviously not going to Eura," her mother said with a laugh. "But this money won't hurt. We can finally replace that leaky old kayak."

Anuqi's father put a hand on her shoulder. She wanted to shrug it off, but didn't resist.

"I'm sorry, Anuqi," he said. "You must know there's

no way this could lead to Suka. You're going to have to accept that she's gone."

At that, Anuqi pulled away. "Suka is out there," she snapped. "We lost her once to the Greencloaks, and you just let her go then. Now we have a second chance to make things right, and you want to give up on her?"

Her mother's shoulders slumped, and her father just sighed. Anuqi knew she couldn't expect them to understand.

"Suka left of her own accord," her mother said softly as she tucked the pouch of coins under a wolfskin blanket. "We guarded her for years, and she walked away—twice. But now that's all over. There's nothing we can do."

"I told you that girl did something to her!" Anuqi protested. "I *saw* it!"

"We're all devastated that Suka is gone," her father added. "But can't you see what this is, Anuqi? Someone is trying to take advantage of you."

"I'm going to go check the snares," Anuqi said, grabbing her parka and roughly pushing the tent flaps back. She stepped out and shrugged the parka over her shoulders. She'd already visited the snares—she didn't really need to check them until the morning—but Anuqi wanted space to breathe.

As she trudged through the snow, an icy wind blew across the tundra. She really should have brought snowshoes, but there was no way she was going back now. Anuqi leaned into the wind's biting caress. Suka's power was in that Arctican chill, and when she let it envelop her, Anuqi could sense that, somewhere, Suka was still out there. For a moment she stopped and hugged herself, as her body reached out for a connection that she knew was dead. A wave of answering pain blossomed in her chest.

The message probably *was* a lie, but her parents were still wrong. One way or another, Anuqi would find her spirit animal again.

As she walked, she felt the wind tugging at her. It gusted, twisting through the hills like a roar. Almost like the roar of a polar bear.

Anuqi glanced up at the sky, where the aurora was beginning to appear—green brushes of light against the starry sky. The legends of the Ardu held that the aurora's lights were the spirits of her ancestors, playing in the sky forever. Perhaps her grandmother was up there, looking down on her plight. And, knowing Grandmother, probably also muttering curses at outsiders and demanding that Anuqi peel her some fireweed to soothe her gums. But still, she would be watching.

The wind roared. Anuqi knew what she had to do.

When she returned to the family tent, her parents had already gone to sleep. Anuqi had suffered through their snoring, his low-pitched and hers high, for all her life. Now, whatever else happened, at least she would have a break from that.

Creeping with a stealth honed by prowling through the tundra and avoiding predators, Anuqi gathered up traveling clothes, snowshoes, food, and her trusty snow knife. She would never truly feel safe again until she had Suka back, but the knife strapped against her thigh made her feel slightly better.

It was the work of a moment to pull back the wolf-skin that her mother hid all her valuables behind. Finally, Anuqi piled up old skins so that it would look like she was in her bed if anyone checked.

The low-pitched snoring stopped for a moment. Anuqi froze, her heart pounding like seal-leather drums in her ears. If her parents woke up and discovered her, they would never let her out of their sight again.

But then her father sneezed, and his snoring resumed. Anuqi slipped out of her parents' tent like a soft night breeze and started away.

At the edge of the village, she strapped on her snow-shoes. With the night's head start, she would be too far gone for anyone to catch her. And with the wind gusting steadily and a light snow falling, tracking her would be difficult to impossible.

As she started out across the snow, Anuqi looked up. The aurora was in full force now, greens and blues spilling across the sky. This outsider might be another liar, but she was determined. The dull ache where Suka had been was still there, but somehow slightly less as she tracked across the tundra. One way or another, she was going to find her spirit animal. Anuqi would not return to the lands of the Ardu until they were reunited.

Anuqi left her snowshoes behind when she reached the Arctican channel, and packed her thick parka away when the ferryman's boat touched down on Eura's northern shores. The trek was long, and more than a few copper coins had been lost to innkeepers' hands just to get directions. By the time she reached Radenbridge, Anuqi's bag was empty.

Radenbridge was not a large town by Euran standards, but it was easily several times the size of any of the settlements in Ardu lands. Even in her lightest hide clothes, Anuqi was too warm, and she felt out of place amid the crowds of pale foreigners.

Except I'm the foreigner here, she realized with a grimace. *Not them.*

The Smiling Fox Inn was not hard to find, right on the main thoroughfare. She dodged wagons and a stray dog as she crossed the street to the largest building in town. It was marked with a red fox that was grinning as if it had just raided all the chicken coops Anuqi had seen on farms along the road.

She glanced up as she approached the inn. The sun was still out, but she had been watching the skies. It was the last day of the waning moon. Ignoring the stares of the passing Eurans, she pushed open the door and walked in.

The inn's common room was the largest building she had ever been inside, two stories tall with tables and benches strewn across the stone floor. She stood frozen for a moment as the patrons bustled around her, calling for food and drink.

A small man appeared at her shoulder, wearing a stained apron and a perpetually annoyed expression.

"Come, come, you're drawing attention," he said, taking her by the elbow and guiding her to a dark table in the corner. "Just sit here. I'll bring you some soup."

"I don't have any money left, so—" she started, but the man hushed her.

"Just sit here," he repeated firmly. "I'll bring you everything you need."

She nodded, grateful to finally be off her feet after the long journey. And with no coin left, she hadn't had any real food in a day. She was famished.

The man brought her a bowl of steaming-hot stew, which Anuqi attacked with vigor. When she picked up the bowl to drain the last dregs of broth, she noticed a small piece of paper folded underneath the bowl. As stealthily as she could, Anuqi grabbed the paper and held it below the table, straining to read it in the flickering firelight.

She stared at the markings on the sheet. They looked scratched, like they had been scrawled by one of the chickens in a panic before the smiling fox arrived. Of course, it wouldn't have mattered if the note had been gorgeously penned by the head scribe to the Queen of Eura; she still wouldn't be able to read it.

She stared at the page. Why had she come so far, for a "friend" who didn't even know that most Arcticans couldn't read? And now she was stuck. She didn't have enough coin to afford the passage back home, even if she could make it that far.

When the innkeeper returned again, she was still looking at the piece of paper in her lap.

"What are you doing?" he hissed. "You're starting to draw attention to yourself, as if you hadn't already."

She glared at him. "I can't read this," she hissed back, feeling the color rise in her face at having to admit that.

He rolled his eyes but leaned in close and whispered in her ear. "It says to go to the top floor, to the last door on the right, and knock four times," he said. "Now, get out of here and forget you ever spoke to me."

Anuqi nodded sullenly.

"That skinny shrew didn't pay me nearly enough for this," he muttered as he walked away.

Anuqi waited for a minute, pretending to pack up her few possessions. Then she made her way up the stairs. She tried to put on her best casual walk, but wondered as she mounted the stairs if that was just making it worse. There had never been a call for trickery and lies among the Ardu, other than coming up with the occasional excuse for why she was out with Suka too long.

Suka . . . Anuqi tried to put her friend out of her thoughts as she reached the top floor. Was there some chance she would find out where her spirit animal was? Would this "friend" be able to help get Suka back? Probably not. But she'd come this far. Anuqi knocked four times.

The door swung open a crack. A beady eye and the point of a crossbow peered out. Anuqi stepped back and gasped, but the door opened fully and the crossbow was lowered. The eye belonged to a tall young woman with thin cheekbones. The girl glanced up and down the hallway with sharp movements, and then motioned Anuqi inside.

Anuqi stepped in. The room was bare and basic, much like the ones she'd stayed in on her journey through Eura to get here. There was a chest, a rug, and a modest straw bed. Sitting on the corner of the bed was a tiny boy.

The young woman closed the door and cleared her throat. "Thank you for coming. We weren't sure if you would believe the note."

Anuqi said nothing. Had she believed it? She had almost wanted to, but it just seemed too far-fetched.

"I'm Talon, and this is Grif," the girl said.

Anuqi eyed the two of them. The young woman looked frail, and the boy was tiny. She groaned. She knew the note had been too good to be true. "You two? You're going to help get my spirit animal back? What, you and the eight-year-old over there?"

"Hey, I may look eight, but I'm actually eleven, and I punch like I'm fifteen." He held up a tiny fist, making his best menacing face.

The girl who called herself Talon started laughing, high-pitched and flighty, and Anuqi couldn't help but chuckle herself. The boy scowled at first, then grinned. He hopped down from the bed and performed a mock bow.

"Grif Burnam, at your service," he said, straightening up to his unimpressive full height. He was wearing a gray cape and had two tiny daggers sheathed at his belt.

"You . . . you look like the world's smallest adventurer,"

Anuqi couldn't help but say. She had to admit, he was almost cute, with his tiny battle gear and determined face.

"And what if I am?" The boy raised his chin, gaining perhaps a quarter inch in height. "I go places others can't go. I see things others can't see. I'm the one," he said, practically glowing with pride, "who found out who would be in Radenbridge this week. And with stolen spirit animals in tow."

Anuqi glared at the tiny boy. "Do you mean that Suka is here? In Radenbridge?"

"No," Talon interrupted softly. "I'm sorry, Anuqi, she's not here. But the girl who helped Zerif steal her from you is. And she has other spirit animals, stolen from others like you."

"So you brought me all this way, but you don't know where Suka is? You want me for something completely different?"

Talon sighed. "Zerif's power is growing. We have to fight him any way we can. If we keep harrying him, we hope to discover more of his plans and methods. When we learn enough, hopefully we'll be able to find your spirit animals and rescue them. Until then, we'll strip him of his allies. But we need your assistance."

"Help us, and my daggers will be sworn to your service," Grif said, puffing his little chest out. "I will help rescue your spirit animal, or die trying."

Anuqi stifled a laugh.

"He's serious," Talon said, nervously checking the window and listening at the door for a moment. The girl seemed to be always in motion.

"Why do you even care?" Anuqi asked, raising an eyebrow at Grif. "What's in this for you?"

Grif's confidence suddenly sagged, just for a moment. Then he straightened up.

"There were strangers in town the day I summoned my spirit animal," he said. "There are no Nectar Ceremonies anymore, so it just happened out of the blue—the sky darkened and there was this flash of light. Zerif struck before anyone realized what was happening. Our Greencloak was an old man; he went down immediately. My father was slashed across the chest, and the other adults ran away. I hid and watched. Zerif took him. Zerif used that weird worm and took my spirit animal. I never even got to touch him."

"I'm sorry," Anuqi said automatically. Something about the way he said it, so calm and tight, made her believe him even more than if he'd started bawling. "I . . . I know what that's like."

"Grif summoned Arax the Ram," Talon said with a sad smile. "Another reincarnated Great Beast. Zerif and Raisha stole him away, just as they did Suka, and two others before them. Now do you see why we have to fight? They will continue taking spirit animals, unless they're stopped."

Anuqi shook her head. It was all too much. Grif, with his tiny daggers, was about as threatening as a baby seal. And Talon looked as if a stiff breeze would blow her out to sea. If Anuqi joined forces with them, she was likely to get hurt or killed. And then what would happen to Suka?

Even so . . . Anuqi noted that Grif did seem to wear his weapons with a certain confidence. And Talon's crossbow was still loaded and cocked, even if it was pointing down at the floor. Anuqi had never been a fighter. Ardu children were trained to trap, track, and survive in the cold, but the closest she'd come to fighting was tussling with the other kids in her settlement.

More than ever, Anuqi wished for Suka. Her warmth, her strength . . . and her massive claws. With her polar bear at her side, Anuqi had always felt safe. Like nothing could harm her.

She looked pointedly at the crossbow. "Do I have a choice? Or will you just make me do what you want, like everyone else?"

"You're completely free to go," Talon said, sighing as she unloaded the crossbow and set it on the bed. "I'll never force someone to serve against their will. Those days are in my past."

Was this girl serious? Anuqi could think of only one way to find out.

Anuqi nodded, then stood up and walked out the door without another word. She went down the stairs and waited, perfectly still, listening for the sounds of movement from above. There was nothing.

She weighed her options. She could try to make her way home. With no money left and her parents likely furious with her, that was a bitter prospect. Or she could place her trust in these two oddball characters and their mission.

Anuqi breathed in deep. She'd come this far. She would have to try, at least.

A moment later she was back up the stairs, knocking on the door.

Talon opened it, staring at Anuqi in surprise.

Behind her, the boy was laughing. "Told you she'd come back," Grif said.

Anuqi gave him a dark look. "I just needed to know if you would actually let me go. If you were telling the truth."

"Then, by all means. Come in," Talon said, glancing nervously back and forth down the hallway as Anuqi entered.

"How can we hit back at them?" Anuqi asked.

"Raisha is camped outside of town," Talon explained. "She has a whole troop of mercenaries with her. Radenbridge's Greencloak is about to hold a ceremony inviting any children who summoned animals to take the green. There are three this year, with three bright, shiny new spirit animals."

"We think Raisha is going to hide in the crowd," Grif added. "Pretend to be part of a merchant's caravan. As soon as the children are all called up, her men will strike."

"And we do what?" Anuqi asked, incredulous. "Take on a whole troop of mercenaries by ourselves? Shouldn't those cursed Greencloaks be taking care of this?"

"The Greencloaks are too far away," Talon explained. "The Keeper and a whole party of them are headed toward Brecksbury, a day's journey from here. But they won't arrive until tomorrow. Plus . . ." Talon faltered, suddenly awkward.

"Talon's got some kind of history with them," Grif said. "I'm guessing she was a criminal, but she doesn't talk about it." He raised his hands in the air, as if talking about an errant puppy.

Anuqi glanced at the wiry girl. That would explain her nervousness. Anuqi wasn't sure she wanted to work with a former criminal, but she didn't say anything. Instead, she just shrugged. "Hey, I'm no friend of the Greencloaks," she said. "When they need you they're all high-minded and virtuous. And then they leave behind a trail of destruction. Just strangers bringing sorrow. And when I could have actually used their help, they were nowhere to be seen."

Talon gave a tight smile and bobbed her head quickly, like a bird. "I know about what happened to the Ardu. My plan should help prevent the same disaster from happening to Radenbridge."

Grif lay a hand on his dagger, which to Anuqi was one half menacing and one half adorable. "Raisha won't know what hit her."

"All right," Anuqi said with a sigh. "I'm in. How are we possibly going to pull this off?"

"Have a seat, and we'll explain everything. We don't have much time to make our preparations."

Anuqi sat cross-legged on the floor, and the three set to work.

The Radenbridge town square was alive with activity. A crowd had gathered, filling it to the brim and overflowing into the streets. Vendors hawked their wares, and a large stage had been set up at the center.

Radenbridge was a market town, and in addition to the presentation, this was a market day. Livestock of all kinds milled about. There were cows, sheep, goats, horses, and other animals tethered all around the square. Cages filled with chickens, geese, and pigeons were lined up near the stage. Animal calls and the clacking of hooves on cobbles filled the air with a strange sort of song.

Talon had given Anuqi new clothes to wear: a woolen cloak and a slouching hat that obscured her features. With her head downcast, she looked like just another farmer or shepherd in from the hills surrounding Radenbridge.

Anuqi let herself be pushed back and forth by the crowd, slowly working her way through the swell to the back of the stage. It wasn't much different from working the waves in a kayak, even if the number of people around her made the hairs on her neck stand on end.

She cast her eyes over the crowd, trying to note who looked suspicious. There were no mysterious cloaked figures, but there were certainly plenty of tough-looking men who could easily be mercenaries.

Then, at the edge of the square, Anuqi saw her: Raisha. The girl seemed to be enjoying bossing around a pair of burly mercenaries. She had a slight sneer on her face, the same expression she'd worn as she ripped Suka out of Anuqi's life. A vicious-looking dagger was sheathed at her waist.

The Arctican girl turned away, smiling tightly to herself. If nothing else, Talon and Grif had given her the chance to fight back. Even if their plan seemed unlikely to succeed.

Anuqi kept her head down as Radenbridge's mayor gave a brief speech and the town's Greencloak stepped forward. She didn't dare look back at Raisha. If she was recognized, the whole plan could be ruined.

Radenbridge's Greencloak was a middle-aged man. He might have once been a competent warrior, but now he sported a paunch and moved with ungainly steps. He wouldn't be much help. Anuqi shook her head. The Greencloaks sounded good in the stories, but the reality of them never quite matched up.

"We no longer have the Nectar of Ninani," the mayor said. "But some among you have summoned spirit animals all the same. Come forward!"

A boy was the first to come, with a large yak trotting next to him. It turned when they arrived at the front, eyeing the crowd suspiciously. Then it gave a grunt and leaned down to explore a patch of grass sprouting from between the cobblestones.

Anuqi's body tensed. A tall girl came forward, with a tree frog sitting on her shoulder. A horsefly flitted past and the frog's tongue whipped out and plucked a snack from the air.

Finally a third child, a slight girl with black pigtails, came forward. Her parents had to push her out of the crowd. She vaulted the steps quickly, then took up a position almost behind the taller girl. A Great Dane padded along next to her, looking almost as spooked by the crowd.

Anuqi pushed her way through the press of bodies. The Greencloak stepped forward.

"You have summoned animals and are counted among the Marked. Will you accept the call of the Greencloaks, and serve—"

The chaos erupted before he could finish.

As she charged forward, Anuqi could see and hear it around her: swords screeching out of their scabbards and panicked screaming from all directions. Anuqi caught a glimpse of Raisha in the crowd, her face the very picture of shocked innocence. Anuqi felt a fresh spike of hatred for the unctuous girl.

As the mercenaries advanced from the crowd and the Radenbridge locals fled, Talon emerged from under the stage, grabbing the first boy and girl and their spirit animals and pulling them with her.

The local constable and the Greencloak had drawn their weapons. Anuqi darted past them. The square suddenly exploded as Grif flashed onto the scene, moving faster than Anuqi could have imagined. Grif slashed the leads of the horses and the knots holding the birdcages closed. Everywhere he went, clouds of feathers and beating hooves followed.

"For Arax!" he yelled as he sliced a knot and a stallion charged past.

The panicked animals stampeded through the square, turning confusion into complete pandemonium. Anuqi dodged a crazed mule and reached the girl with the pigtails, the final one to summon an animal.

Anuqi looked down at the girl in front of her. Her eyes were wide, her arms wrapped around the Great Dane's neck.

"Come with me. We have to get you out of here," Anuqi said.

"But who are you?"

"I'm . . . a friend." Anuqi realized with a jolt that this was the same thing that Talon had said to *her*. The word that she'd had such a hard time accepting. "I can help you. I can get you out of here before those men take you. If you will trust me."

Please, Anuqi thought. *Let this girl be more ready to trust than I was.*

For a long moment, the girl shrank back. Anuqi reached out her hand, trying to put the concern she felt into her eyes. Then, reluctantly, the girl took Anuqi's hand. They ran together, dodging chickens, geese, and an irate goat.

Anuqi glanced back as she ran. The last thing she saw before rounding a corner was the town's Greencloak holding off two of Raisha's mercenaries by himself with deft swings from a long sword. Perhaps there was more to him than she'd initially thought.

As her feet pounded on the cobblestones and she pulled the girl along beside her, Anuqi hoped he would make it out alive. The Greencloak was buying them precious seconds.

Around the corner, they caught up to Talon and the two other children. The girl with the tree frog held her spirit animal close, while Talon and the boy were trying to get the yak moving forward. It was slow to start, but with the boy urging it on, it was trotting along by the time Anuqi caught up.

"Let's go!" Anuqi shouted. The odd mix of humans and animals accelerated down the cobbled street.

At the next turn, Grif emerged from an alley grinning like a madman, his face covered in mud.

"Their horses?" Talon asked.

"Cut loose, spooked, and headed for the hills," he answered, sliding easily into their pace.

They reached the town gate, where the guards were struggling to lower the portcullis without much success.

"There's a rock in the gears!" Talon shouted brightly as they charged through. The guards watched in shock as the crowd of people and animals passed them by. Anuqi looked back as they sprinted across the field outside the walls, and saw the gate lowering to the ground.

"Told you it would work," Grif crowed as they reached the trees. There was a sudden crash. "I also loosened the screws on the winch," he added. "Once it starts down, there's no stopping it."

There was shouting at the gate as the mercenaries reached it, only to find it closed. That would buy Anuqi and the others time to make their escape. Anuqi had to admit, she was shocked that their plan had succeeded so far. Maybe Talon and Grif really were capable of pulling this off. Though she still wasn't sure what they were up to.

Anuqi took the lead as they reached the edge of the woods. There was a light dusting of snow on the ground that had fallen overnight.

She led them off the road immediately, heading up a tiny deer trail for a few minutes and then into the deep brush. At least here, horses wouldn't be able to follow.

While Talon and Grif had prepared their tricks in the city, Anuqi had been plotting out their escape path. She might not be much of a fighter, but when it came to tracking and making their way through the snowy landscape, she would wager she knew more than any of these city dwellers.

It was winter and the ground was frozen, but even so she knew they were leaving tracks in the snow that Raisha and her goons would be able to follow.

"What's your name?" Anuqi asked the pigtailed girl.

"I'm Maena," the girl answered. "My family runs the town's mill. Will . . . will I be able to go back to them?"

"You'll need to stay hidden," Talon said. "But once Raisha and these mercenaries have passed, they won't come back. Raisha is a prominent merchant's daughter. She has too much to lose for a few animals."

Anuqi knew what that meant. For normal spirit animals.

For the reborn Great Beasts, like those she and Grif had summoned, Raisha and Zerif would likely never stop hunting—not until they had them all.

Anuqi led them through the woods and a quarter mile down a shallow winter stream before they crossed to the other side.

"My feet are freezing," Maena complained.

"Moving water makes it hard for the trackers to follow us," Anuqi told her. "They'll have to track up and down both sides of the stream looking for signs. This should gain us enough time."

"Raisha is a pampered brat," Talon added. "And she's from southern Zhong, so I doubt she's very familiar with snowy terrain like this. But her mercenaries are experienced hunters. They'll know how to track us."

Anuqi stopped them when they reached a rocky slope, which was mostly free of snow. There would be no tracks left here. She beckoned the three village children and their animals to a large boulder with a hollow behind it.

"This is a good spot to lay low," Anuqi said, pulling aside a thicket of branches that had been covered by snow. Yesterday, Anuqi had carefully prepared it after discussing the plans with Talon and Grif. Once the branches, snow, and leaves were replaced, anyone inside would be almost invisible.

"Hide in here," Anuqi ordered. "Once they pass you, wait an hour then head back downstream."

"We'll take care of Raisha's people," Talon said. "But for now you need to stay out of sight."

The three looked back at Talon, wide-eyed.

"You can do this," Talon assured them.

Maena nodded, then stepped forward and wrapped Anuqi in a hug. "Thank you," the girl said. Her Great Dane barked at them. It wasn't quite the warm furry embrace of Suka, but Anuqi squeezed her back.

"You'll be okay," she whispered. "Don't worry."

Once the three were huddled in the hollow behind the boulder, Anuqi covered the opening and used the branch of a fir tree to brush the snow smooth around them.

Grif picked up a pile of sticks that were lying by the rocks. He handed a pair to Talon and a pair to Anuqi. Anuqi took a look at the bottoms of hers. They were carved into the rough shape of yak hooves.

"We'll need to walk slowly and leave extra prints for a bit," Anuqi instructed Grif and Talon as they set out. "If they stay focused on our trail, they won't realize half of their prey have escaped."

"We'll see who the predators are . . . and who are the prey," Grif said darkly. His right hand squeezed his dagger.

As they walked, they pressed the sticks that Grif had carved yesterday into the snow along their path. Hopefully Raisha would see only that they had stopped briefly, and the humans and animals had all continued up the ravine.

"I knew your skills would be useful, Anuqi," Talon said with a grim smile as they ascended to the top of the ravine, stepping heavily. "You may not be a fighter, but you've a cunning to you."

Anuqi said nothing, but the thought warmed her. She would need all of that cunning in order to eventually rescue Suka.

They kept moving through the evening and into the night. Anuqi used every trick the Ardu hunters taught her—backtracking, circling around, and hopping on rocks—to try to obscure their trail. But they would always leave a few "mistaken" broken branches or tracks.

"Let's not be too good at this," Talon said with a chuckle as she intentionally put a few extra footprints along the way. "We're trying to slow them down, not lose them entirely."

The moon rose as they crossed open farmland. They first saw their pursuers at the edge of a sheep pasture. The figures were distant, barely specks on the horizon. But as the night wore on, the moon made its way across the sky and the shadows shifted on the snow—and the mercenaries kept gaining.

"I'm sorry," Grif said, starting to puff as they moved along. The boy finally seemed to be losing stamina. Running around like he had in the city, Anuqi was only surprised he'd lasted this long. "I won't be the cause of your deaths—let me stay behind. I can slow them down so that you can make it close enough to use the horn."

Anuqi glared at him. "You're not getting off that easy. Stuff your honor."

"Keep moving," Talon shot. "We're close now." She touched the horn around her neck. "Another mile and the Greencloaks will come running."

Anuqi looked behind them. She could make out the individual figures now, their weapons gleaming in the moonlight. She kept her legs moving underneath her, trying to ignore the chill seeping in through her soaked feet and wind-tossed face.

With every step the mercenaries grew closer. Part of Anuqi wanted them to catch up. Let them take their best shot. She had her snow knife buckled at her hip. If she went down fighting, at least she wouldn't have to worry about the emptiness inside her where Suka had been. She could make Raisha pay for what she'd done.

Grif fell behind. Anuqi was about to urge him on when she saw the furious expression on his face as sweat dripped from his hair, even in the cold air. He was already giving it everything.

Finally, breathing heavily, Talon skidded to a stop at the bottom of a ridge amid a stand of trees. She pulled the horn over her neck and held it for a long moment.

"We're here. . . . I just need a moment . . . to catch my breath," she said.

Anuqi took a long look back across the field, where the enemy was approaching. They had gotten so close! If Talon was right, a large force of Greencloaks were camped just over the rise.

Now that they were closing in, Anuqi noticed something alarming about the mercenaries: Raisha wasn't among them.

Her whole body tensed as she searched. There, over to the right, just a stone's throw from their tracks, was another set in parallel. Anuqi spun around just in time to see a figure stepping out of the trees.

Before she could open her mouth, Raisha was behind Talon. A sharp dirk gleaming at Talon's throat.

"Drop the horn," Raisha commanded. Talon let it fall to the ground.

"Grif, Anuqi," Talon said. "Run. It doesn't matter if I die."

"Move an inch and I slit her throat," Raisha said, a cruel grin spreading across her face.

Grif's daggers were out, but he stood unmoving. "If

you hurt her," he said, glaring at Raisha, "you *will* feel my daggers."

Anuqi stood frozen for a moment. Was she really going to let herself be captured for someone she'd only just met? Talon had told her to run.

Anuqi finally spun and started up the hill, but it was too late. The mercenaries had crossed the pasture and were already in the trees, weapons drawn. Anuqi only made it a few steps before one of them crashed into her, sending her staggering. Her foot caught under a root and Anuqi went down, yelping with pain.

She tried to fight back as the mercenaries tied her hands, but her ankle throbbed with every movement. Finally she gave in and let them tie her.

"I'd make you tell me where those spirit animals are, but we don't have time for another wild chase," Raisha said. "Still, I'm sure that Zerif will enjoy questioning you when we meet with him. You have other friends out there, don't you?" she asked Talon.

Talon's sharp features were set. Anuqi had never seen the girl so still.

One of the larger mercenaries hefted Anuqi onto his shoulder as if she weighed nothing. She passed out as her ankle was wrenched once again.

The wagon smelled like a barn. It was full of cages, and each contained an animal. There were birds, ferrets, dogs, and even a porcupine. With every bump they hit, the entire array would explode with noise.

Talon, Grif, and Anuqi were in cages as well. These weren't like the cages in the market, wooden affairs tied shut with rope–they were steel and secured with real locks. The mercenaries had forced them to march through the rest of the night and all the next day, before reaching their wagons and imprisoning them in one full of stolen spirit animals. Grif and Talon had taken turns supporting Anuqi and her broken ankle, which had given her a stab of pain with every step.

"I'm sorry," Anuqi said, eyeing the cut on Talon's neck where Raisha's dirk had rested. "I shouldn't have run."

Talon shrugged. "I told you to."

"I guess I paid for it," Anuqi said. The massive swelling of her sprained ankle had gotten worse.

"Enough of that!" Grif hissed. "Let's figure out how to get out of here."

They each tested the locks and bars of their cages. Anuqi pushed, rattled, and prodded, but there was no give to their prisons. Talon appeared to be making friends with a robin in a nearby cage, but it was just as stuck as they were.

Talon pointed at a pile of weapons and gear in the corner near Anuqi. "Can you reach any of that?"

Anuqi stretched her hand out through the bars of her cage but couldn't get to them.

"What about that pouch at the end?" Grif said. "Maybe it has something small that we could pick the locks with? A sword won't be much use, inside a metal cage."

Anuqi strained, but it was a few handbreadths too far. "Sorry, my arms just aren't long enough," she said.

"Hold on," Talon said. She reached through the metal bars of her enclosure to the robin's small wooden cage and snapped a few of the spokes. The bird hopped free.

"These are spirit animals," Talon explained. "Smarter than most animals."

Through a combination of pointing, nodding, and whispered instructions, Talon was able to convince the robin to flutter over and drag the pouch the few feet required so that Anuqi could reach out and grab it.

The pouch contained flint, a ring of steel, and a gray powder that Anuqi didn't recognize.

"Hold it up to the light," Talon instructed, peering through the bars. "It looks like Zhongese blast powder!" she said at last. "If you light it off by your lock, it should blast it off. Then you can make a run for safety."

It was worth a shot. Anuqi shifted her weight to get started and her ankle twisted again. Pain blazed up and down her leg. She looked down despondently. She could blow the lock and run, but how far would she get trying to sneak away on a sprained ankle?

"Let *me* go," Grif said quietly. "I'll come back for both of you. I swear it on my honor. And on Arax and Suka." He scuttled forward in his cage, looking at her with big, serious eyes. "Trust me. I won't fail you."

Anuqi sat still, considering. She'd tried to escape alone once already, and look where it had gotten her.

She looked from Talon to Grif, sizing up the willowy young woman and the tiny warrior. Her companions weren't much to look at, but together the three of them had already saved several spirit animals. Three kids wouldn't have to feel the cold emptiness that had been sucking at Anuqi every moment since Suka had gone. Perhaps the time had come to put some faith in her new friends.

She untied the powder and tossed it over to Grif. It was the work of a moment for him to put the blast powder inside his lock. Talon tossed him an old letter that she had hidden in her shirt, which Grif lit after several attempts.

He waited until the wagon hit another large bump, then lit the blast powder as the wagon shook and the animals went wild. The tiny explosion was muffled by the cacophony.

Grif coughed, waving smoke away. What was left of his lock hung flimsily on the cage door. Grif prodded it with the steel striker, and the charred lump of metal fell to the wagon floor.

He was out of his cage in an instant. Grif grabbed an ax from the pile of supplies. A few blows to the floor-boards, timed with the wagon's bumps, revealed the dark ground passing by below.

"Wait until you see a mud puddle," Anuqi suggested. "Your clothes are brown and dirty, so you should blend in. If polar bears use snow cover to hunt, you should be able to use mud cover to stay hidden."

"Take that robin with you," Talon suggested. "The Greencloaks should be able to recognize a stolen spirit animal. Our only chance now is to find them."

Grif carefully grabbed the tiny bird and waited until a large mud puddle passed by, then dropped through the hole into the brown muck. Anuqi and Talon listened closely for several minutes, but there were no shouts of alarm or sounds of combat. Had he escaped?

Anuqi's stomach twisted on itself as the night passed slowly. She hoped she'd done the right thing in letting Grif go.

She closed her eyes and imagined herself dropping through that hole, leaving all this behind.

Through the cracks in the wagon, they could just see dawn breaking. The sound of a horn echoed in the morning air. Anuqi was tired and groggy, and only slowly recognized the noise for what it was—a war horn.

"The Greencloaks are here," Talon said softly. Anuqi would have expected her to sound more pleased that they were being rescued.

Shortly after, the shouts of men and women and the crashing of steel on steel rang out, accompanied by animal calls of all kinds. Two errant arrows slammed into the walls of their wagon.

Talon and Anuqi waited silently, not knowing what to hope for.

"If it's the Greencloaks who find us," Talon said, "tell them you never met me. Tell them you were captured separately. It will go easier for you that way."

Anuqi wanted to ask why, but the set of Talon's lips made it clear that she had said all she would say. Anuqi gripped the bars of her cage as the battle continued outside.

Suddenly, a tiny head popped up through the hole in

the floor of the wagon. A small, muddy figure wriggled his way up inside.

"Told you I'd be back," Grif said with a grin. "And look what I grabbed off one of the mercenaries!" He brandished a ring of keys and set to work trying them on Anuqi's cage. A moment later, all three of them were free.

"Let's get out now, while they're still fighting," Talon suggested.

"We should be able to make it to the trees at the side of the road if we're quick," Grif said. "They're fairly distracted, what with the battle and all."

The three slipped down through the hold, shimmied across the ground, and dashed for the woods. Anuqi gritted her teeth as the pain in her ankle flared, but kept running.

As they passed into the darkness of the woods, Anuqi looked back to the train of wagons. Greencloaks and mercenaries were in pitched battle.

"That's the Keeper," Talon said, pointing to a young figure resplendent in tellunum armor, battling two mercenaries. A moment later, the mercenaries gave up and fled for the trees on the other side of the road.

"And over there—that one is Keith." A Greencloak had cornered Raisha and had an arrow nocked on his bow, pointed at Raisha's heart. "Looks like he finally learned how to fight."

Anuqi grinned as she saw Raisha raise her hands in surrender. The other mercenaries were soon dropping their weapons or running for the woods, Greencloaks on their heels.

"Let's keep moving before they realize I'm missing,"

Grif said. "Here, let me help you," he said, slipping under Anuqi's arm to help keep the weight off her ankle.

Anuqi leaned heavily on Grif as they walked, and smiled despite the pain as they slipped deeper into the woods.

"What now?" Grif asked as the sounds of battle faded and they made their way past a snow-covered farm.

"I have some friends I'd like you to meet," Talon answered.

"Friends who will help us find Suka?" Anuqi asked through gritted teeth.

"Yes," Talon said. "We're not as numerous or powerful as the Greencloaks—or whoever Zerif is working for—but we care about Erdas. And we will do whatever it takes to get your spirit animals back."

Anuqi glanced back along the path they'd come. The Greencloaks had looked dashing, swooping in for the rescue like that. But still, she had no desire to spend any more time with them than absolutely necessary, even if they had likely just saved her from a horrible fate at the hands of Zerif.

Let Zerif, Raisha, and the Greencloaks take care of each other, leaving their usual trail of destruction. Anuqi had all the friends she needed.

KOVO

REBEL BOND

By Billy Merrell

"CALM DOWN," THE OLD MONK SAID. BUT TAKODA couldn't. His arms were still shaking from the fight.

"Be calm," Ananda repeated. Her soothing voice was a demonstration of calm, even as she commanded him to be still. Takoda looked up into her soft brown eyes, hoping she couldn't hear the pounding in his chest.

He hated being told to calm down, as if the anger he felt was something he could control. As if he was wrong to feel outrage or hate after everything that had happened.

Ananda told Takoda to take a deep breath. She rested a graceful hand on his shoulder, so gently he could barely feel it. He closed his eyes and breathed. Slowly his trembling subsided, but the bruises on his left cheek and right fist felt suddenly sore.

"Takoda," Ananda said. "You can't keep picking fights."

He wanted to defend himself, to tell Ananda that it wasn't him who started it this time. But that wasn't entirely the truth.

Takoda couldn't honestly remember what Sudo had even said. But he could remember the cruel face the boy had made as he teased Takoda. Sudo's tongue had stuck out and his brow furrowed, as if the air itself tasted sour. His chapped lips had twisted into a sneer—and then gaped in surprise when Takoda leaped to defend himself.

Ananda glanced down at Takoda's saffron robe, and her stoic, regal face gave way to disappointment. When he looked down, he realized the fabric was badly torn.

If Father was here, he could mend it, he thought bitterly. If he still had a father, he wouldn't be here, getting in fights.

And then he thought of his mother, who was as beautiful and patient as Ananda was—but strong, too. Willing to fight for a good cause—like marrying a Zhongese man even though she was Niloan. Willing to go into battle against the Conquerors for their family.

Takoda squeezed his eyelids as tightly as he could, afraid of what would happen if he opened them.

He expected to be punished for what he'd done—Ananda was in charge of disciplining the acolytes, after all—but the gentle monk pulled him close instead. Takoda instinctively wanted to pull away, but stopped himself. It felt nice, listening to her breathing and imagining a future in which he might be as peaceful as Ananda.

"What would you have done," she asked gently, "if you were at home?" Ananda let go, holding Takoda at arm's length and looking him in the eyes.

It was the first time since Takoda arrived at the monastery that any of the monks had mentioned the home he'd lost. He gaped at her, too busy thinking about the question to piece together an answer.

"When you were upset about something, what would you have done then?" Ananda waited patiently.

"I would have run," he confessed. Takoda thought about the savannahs that circled his village in southern Nilo, and how the shallow grass whipped in the wind for as far as the eye could see. He remembered how the combination of sweat and speed cooled his dark skin, even in the full sun. Being out in the grass helped clear his mind, helped him forget everything but the pace of his feet against the earth and the drum of his pulse in the air. He imagined the sky itself could hear his heart. The birds sang to its beat as they dipped close, as if cheering him on.

"I would have run until I couldn't run anymore," Takoda said.

The deep creases around Ananda's eyes softened, and Takoda wondered if she wasn't as nostalgic for wide open spaces as he was. She led them to sit together on the cool steps.

Surrounded by stone and sky, the temple was several miles from the closest field. Takoda knew because he had scanned the landscape from each of the monastery's many majestic towers. It was perched on the rocky shore of a deep river, water to one side, forest on the other. Nowhere to run.

"Have you met Nambi?" Ananda asked, rolling up the stiff sleeve of her blue robe. Takoda shook his head. "Takoda, meet Nambi. Nambi, meet Takoda. I think you'll be friends."

There, on Ananda's slender brown arm, rested the bold tattoo of a giraffe, sitting patiently with its legs folded under. "Nambi loves to run, too. And so do I," Ananda explained. "But this monastery is no place for a giraffe, is it?" She was right, and the fact seemed to bring her great pain.

"So why are you here?" Takoda asked her, wondering how long Nambi had been forced to wait in passive state.

"To heal," the old woman said. "Same as you. Sometimes it's necessary for a person to be away from their place of comfort for a time. Nambi will run again soon. And so will you, Takoda."

Ananda rolled her sleeve back down and stood. She looked off toward the horizon, to where the sun hovered low in the sky. Takoda caught himself smiling as he looked up at her. He realized it had been a very long time since he'd smiled.

"As for your punishment . . ." she began.

Takoda's heart sank as he remembered the trouble he was in.

"You will take over Sudo's post in the west tower. Starting right now." She pointed toward an entryway, beyond which stood the first shadowy steps of a *very* long climb. Takoda's eyes scanned the outer walls of the tower, up to where a distant belfry stood among the clouds.

"Three strikes," Ananda said. "You'd better hurry."

Takoda nodded, unable to look at her. He did as he was told, scurrying toward the entrance.

Peering up the spiral, he looked to where the highest stairs disappeared into darkness. Each of the ancient stone steps was worn down in the center, leaving a rounded impression so that no step was completely flat. Takoda couldn't help but wonder how many young monks had climbed the staircase before him, wearing a curve like that into the stone with nothing but their sandals. And all to ring a bell as the sun hit the horizon. Once at dawn, once at sunset.

Takoda hadn't run in over a year now. Even brief trips up and down stairs left him winded. He briefly wondered if he was up for the challenge. Hurrying, Takoda tried to count the steps as he took them.

It wasn't the same as running, but Takoda caught himself in a familiar pace. The soles of his sandals hit each second step in time, and his increasingly loud breaths echoed against the dark stones. Up and up and up.

Takoda thought of Sudo climbing. The bully's broad forehead creasing, covered with beads of sweat. At first it made Takoda angry, that what was once Sudo's punishment was now his own. But then Takoda managed to leave his annoyance behind, climbing past it up the spiral.

The boy's mind wandered to the savannah, and the sweet sting of the grass at his ankles. Up and up, Takoda thought of his home and of the feeling of exhaustion as he had returned from a run. His father would bring him water, not saying a word about where he had gone until he had been ready to speak. And his mother would watch on, a strange look of pride on her slender face.

Up and up and ever up, he climbed. When Takoda lost count, he refused to let it slow him down. Instead, he simply started over again from zero.

He thought of the last time he had seen each of his parents. Before the war ripped his family away, he remembered his mother waking him in the night to say good-bye. She had kissed his forehead, her braids pulled tightly back and her chest covered with armor. Takoda remembered it had hurt to hug her, the hard metal pressing against his chest.

His mother never came home.

Takoda thought of his father on the last morning he ever saw him. The Devourer's army was sweeping across Nilo. He remembered the fire in his father's eyes as he burned down their modest hut, hoping to trick the enemy into moving on without searching for survivors.

And then, finally, Takoda recalled his gentle father's deep-throated scream as the two of them were discovered hiding in the wreckage, covered in soot.

Up and up, Takoda remembered his father's last words as he commanded the boy to run. "Don't stop until you can't see smoke," he had said.

And Takoda hadn't stopped.

And he had survived.

He'd watched the horizon from the safety of trees on the far side of the savannah. He watched for a long time, afraid to close his eyes, until they began to twitch and tremble. Takoda had watched through the twilight and into the dark, scanning and scanning the shadows for his brave father, realizing he would never come.

Takoda was no longer thinking of climbing when he reached the top of the tower. The sudden brightness of the high windows startled him, like fire catching in his eyes. Pinprick stars speckled his vision as he leaned against the stone and struggled to catch his breath.

Remembering his duty, he found the large mallet hung on the tower wall and timed his first strike so that the first knell rang out deeply just as the sun hit the horizon.

Goooongggg!

Takoda could feel the vibrations on his arms and face. They tingled against his tender cheek. He struck the bell again.

Goooongggg!

This time it was as if the vibrations rang through his very thoughts. Takoda felt suddenly dizzy, as if the tower beneath him was quaking. His vision blurred and the tower seemed to darken all around him. Then—a flash! It was as if the sky had lit up with a flash of noon sun. But only for the briefest moment. In an instant, the light was gone.

Takoda blinked, seeing the same pinprick stars as before. *It must have been a reflection off the bell,* he told himself. But strangely, he sensed something had changed.

He remembered Ananda's instructions. "Three strikes," she had told him. Takoda's stomach twisted into a knot as he realized he'd already messed up the timing of the third toll. Monks all over the monastery must have heard his failure. Two tolls had rung out loud and clear, followed by deafening silence.

Takoda hurriedly lifted the hammer to strike the bell one last time. But as he aimed, he saw a terrifying face reflected in the curve of the metal. Deep-set eyes glared from above a snarling fanged mouth.

Snapping around, he saw that the same red eyes stared wildly at him from the top of the dark stairs.

Run! Takoda thought. But where?

A monster inched toward him from the shadows. As it stepped into the light, its face was revealed by the orange glow of the sunset.

A silverback gorilla.

Takoda hit the bell as hard as he could, hoping to scare the beast away.

Gooooooonnnnnngggg!

But the ape's red eyes stayed fixed on Takoda's. The animal squinted at the boy, pulling itself forward on huge fists. A gust of wind blew through the bell tower, rustling the long black hair on the creature's arms. Each of its biceps were as thick as Takoda's waist.

Goooongggg! Goooongggg! Goooooooonnggggg!

Takoda pounded and pounded the bell, hoping someone would hear the extra tolls as a warning—a call for help. The ape raised a clasping hand, reaching. For Takoda's arm? Or for the mallet? No! It was reaching for the bell. The gorilla pinched the rim with its hairy knuckles, muffling the sound. The knell cut short.

Takoda dropped the hammer, and it crashed by his feet.

"Run!" he heard his father say, but his legs wouldn't move.

Caught in the stare of the ape's red eyes, Takoda suddenly recognized him. There was only one gorilla in the history of Erdas with eyes like that.

Kovo.

All reason told Takoda that it was impossible, but he knew in his gut that he was right.

Suddenly, Takoda didn't want to run. He wanted to fight. Not only to hold his ground, but to hurt Kovo—kill him if he could. The gorilla was responsible for the deaths of his parents, and countless others across Erdas. He had masterminded not one, but *two* great wars.

But what was Kovo doing in the temple's bell tower?

The truth fell on Takoda like the setting of the sun, darkening the world. The strange flash of light . . . The appearance of the ape, not as a gigantic Great Beast, but a normal-sized gorilla . . .

Takoda had summoned a spirit animal, and it was the worst one who'd ever lived.

Even beneath his horror, Takoda felt the connection forming between them, an invisible tether pulling them closer. His skin tingled, and he longed to reach out a hand and touch the ape.

He fought the urge with everything he had.

Not knowing what else to do, Takoda screamed. Right in Kovo's monstrous face, as loudly and for as long as he could. All of the boy's breath seared through his throat in a single, extended blast.

Kovo screamed back instantly. His fanged jaws opened wide as he let out a terrible roar, twice as deep and loud as Takoda's. The boy could feel the ape's wet breath hit his face. Kovo was close enough and strong enough to crush Takoda like a bug if he wanted to, but Takoda went on screaming anyway, the sound all but lost beneath the ape's. Kovo roared, and the boy roared back, until he had nothing left in his lungs.

A dozen monks suddenly piled in, clambering up the stairs. They cast a huge net over the ape, like the ones the fishermen used to dredge the river.

Takoda didn't think it would do much to restrain the gorilla, but amazingly, Kovo didn't fight them. He just stared forward through the thick knots of rope.

Takoda looked around at the alarmed faces of the monks. One by one, they turned from the mysterious ape to Takoda. And when he looked back at Kovo, the ape was watching him, too, with unapologetic red eyes. As if he was figuring out the perfect way to destroy the boy.

"He's a spirit animal now," Ananda said, a hint of wonder in her usually calm voice. "*Your* spirit animal."

The two sat together on the floor. They were in the monastery's granary, a large building full of simple silos that could be locked from the outside. Takoda had been hurried into just such a silo while the monks fetched Ananda.

Elsewhere in the granary, Kovo was locked inside another.

Spirit animal. Takoda couldn't get the words out of his head. His whole life, he had thought he knew what it meant to have one. Now he was no longer sure. What kind of *spirit* did Takoda have to be bonded with such a creature? Kovo was the most villainous, conniving wretch in the history of Erdas.

Takoda shook his head furiously. He didn't want to believe it.

"The pain you described," Ananda said. "The dizziness. That sinking feeling in your gut. It won't go away until your bond is complete. You have to touch him."

"No," he said. "I don't want to. I don't deserve any of this."

"It isn't a punishment, Takoda. It just *is*."

But it felt like a punishment. She was holding him captive, after all, there in one of the stone cells of the granary. The same as Kovo.

"Well, what if I refuse the bond?" he asked Ananda. Takoda couldn't stand the thought of looking into Kovo's bloodred eyes for the rest of his life, knowing what he had done. Besides, what if their bond made Takoda evil, too? What if a life of horror was the boy's destiny? He had to believe he had some choice in the matter.

Kovo began pounding the other side of the stone wall—a sound that had become familiar. It was as if he intended to break the wall apart to get to Takoda. After a while, the pounding subsided, followed by the duller sound of scraping.

How long would it take for Kovo to break down the wall, or to scrape the chains until he was free?

Another wave of pain washed over Takoda. He tried to hide it from Ananda, but she saw the boy's clenched jaw and curling toes. And then a new pain came, at the pit of his stomach. Until he thought he might throw up.

"That's it," Ananda said, standing. "If you won't go to Kovo, I'll bring him to you." Takoda begged her to stop, but Ananda ignored him. She unlatched the heavy granary door. The old hinges shrieked as she pulled it open. Takoda started to follow her, but another spell of dizziness dragged the boy back to the ground. Kovo was beating the wall again, and with every vibration Takoda's head throbbed, as if it was the inside of his skull the ape was pounding.

Takoda could hear Ananda unlatch the door to Kovo's cell. Instantly, the pounding stopped. A moment later, he heard her open the door. But instead of the shrieking of hinges, all Takoda could hear was Ananda's voice, shrieking his name.

Takoda pushed himself up and stood, straining against the knot in his stomach. Kovo had taken away everyone the boy loved. Of course he would try to take Ananda from him too.

But as soon as Takoda passed through the doorway, he was relieved to see that Kovo hadn't hurt her. Instead, Ananda was standing inside the ape's cell, covering her mouth with her two hands. The horror on her face prepared Takoda for the worst, and yet still, when the boy looked into the room, it was as if the stone floor had dropped out from beneath him.

There were bright smears of blood all over the walls, where the gorilla had pounded and scraped his fists. Kovo himself sat placidly in the center of the cell. He was staring at Takoda again, as intensely as he had before. Only now his knuckles were as crimson as his treacherous eyes.

Kovo's eyes. Looking into them, the pain and dizziness subsided. Takoda hated it, but it was as if the ape's terrible gaze was healing him somehow.

Takoda looked away, preferring any pain to even the slightest pang of kinship with the beast. But it was too late. The sickness he felt was nearly gone, replaced by the familiar yearning to reach out and make contact with the animal.

Breathe, he told himself. As he did, the boy's nostrils filled with the metallic smell of blood. Takoda looked around the cell walls, and something puzzled him.

The room was covered in Kovo's blood. But that didn't make any sense. The stories of the ape had always said he was very clever—if Kovo was trying to knock the wall down, he should have pounded the same few stones until they cracked. And yet he'd painted the room with his own blood.

"I'm going to get help," Ananda said, rushing from the room.

When Takoda turned to follow her, Kovo sprang toward him with alarming speed. The gorilla was stopped short, thanks to a heavy chain attached to a collar at his throat. Kovo lifted a fist in Takoda's direction and held it out. More blood seeped from the fresh wounds.

"What do you want?" Takoda asked him furiously. "What more could you possibly want from me?"

But Kovo was no longer looking him in the eyes. He was staring at the boy's clenched fists, dangling at his sides. Kovo glanced at his own fist, then back at Takoda's. Then he turned his hand over, and the fist unfolded into an open palm.

"I'm nothing like . . ." Takoda said to the monster. But the words caught in his throat as he wondered if it was true. His bruised fist was still sore from his fight with Sudo, even though he could barely remember why he had punched him.

"Forget it," Takoda said, turning again to leave. He didn't care if walking away from Kovo made him sick and dizzy. He refused to give his enemy what he wanted.

Kovo pounded the ground and grunted impatiently. When Takoda turned around, the gorilla was scraping the floor with his blood, leaving a half-circle smear on the dirty stone. Kovo looked up at him wildly, and then back at his own fist, still pressed to the ground. Kovo then scraped a zigzag, before staring up at the boy again.

Takoda didn't know what response the ape was waiting for, but when he didn't give it to him, Kovo furrowed his brow. He scraped another zigzag above the first, but it left no blood. The grit from the granary floor had caked onto his wounded knuckles.

Kovo pounded the ground again, until there was fresh blood dripping from the ape's hand. Staring at him hard, Kovo painted a bright zigzag in the exact place he had tried to before.

"It's a drawing," Takoda said, and Kovo nodded.

Looking around the cell walls again, the boy no longer saw only chaotic smears. Instead, he noticed one image repeated again and again. It was of gigantic fanged jaws, wide open, howling, baring teeth—all drawn in Kovo's blood.

Hovering within each gaping mouth was a bloody spiral.

Ananda startled Takoda, setting a bucket of blue-green liquid at his feet. She handed him a rag and ordered him to clean Kovo's wounds.

"He's trying to communicate something to me."

"Of course he is," Ananda said. "You're his human partner."

Takoda wanted so badly for her to be wrong. But he knew already that she wasn't. He could feel the bond forming with Kovo, even without their touching.

And he could feel the difference inside himself. Some inner strength he thought had died with his mother had found its way back to him.

But Kovo is evil, he wanted to say to Ananda. At least, the other Kovo had been. But with the ape staring at Takoda, his bleeding knuckles pressing into the stone, the boy couldn't bring himself to say it.

"Maybe you'll bring out the best in him," Ananda told Takoda gently. And with that she closed the door, leaving him alone with his spirit animal.

Takoda wet the rag with liquid from the bucket, his pulse quickening. He took one step closer to Kovo, then paused. The menacing ape held out a dirty, blood-caked fist. Takoda reached for it slowly with the rag, his hand shaking. Without warning, Kovo snatched the rag out of the boy's hand and threw it to the ground with a splat.

Then Kovo raised his fist out to him again.

Takoda knew what the gorilla was waiting for. And deep down he knew he was waiting for it too. It was as if a spark of energy was humming in the air between them.

Takoda closed his eyes, searching inside himself, desperately trying to commit his own thoughts and feelings to memory—if for no other reason than to know afterward if something had changed.

Takoda reached out and pressed his smaller fist to Kovo's.

The bond with Kovo had formed like skin over an old wound. It hadn't healed the feelings of distrust Takoda had for him. Instead, it had merely buried them, so that Takoda could think of more than death when he looked into Kovo's eyes. So that the boy didn't hear the ape's gibber and think only about his father screaming for him to run.

But when Takoda was startled by a feeling he couldn't place, he realized it might be part of their bond.

That night he woke up in a panic, only to find Kovo staring at him from the corner of his room. The ape had been chained to the wall, though the monks had left some blankets and pillows for him, which sat unused in a pile.

Takoda blinked through the darkness, shaking away the nightmare that had woken him.

"Can you feel me, too?" he asked after a moment. "From your side of the bond?"

Kovo looked away, disinterested. Takoda was starting to suspect that Kovo was even less pleased with their pairing than he himself was.

Kovo pointed to the door impatiently.

"It isn't time to ring the bell yet," Takoda said tiredly, lying back again.

But Kovo grunted and pointed, not letting the boy go back to sleep. Eventually Takoda gave in. He sighed and threw his legs over the bed, then shambled over to Kovo and unlocked his shackles from the wall.

Kovo followed him out the door, toward the west tower. It was early morning, not yet dawn. The ape moved slowly, his two large nostrils taking in the morning forest air as it poured through the monastery. Takoda tried again to engage the ape with questions, but he was almost entirely unresponsive.

The only rise he was able to get out of the gorilla was when Takoda chained him to the foot of the tower. Kovo seemed alarmed that he would leave him behind, and tugged at the iron collar with his bandaged hands.

"You can come with me, if you don't get in my way," Takoda told him. "But you have to hurry."

Kovo snorted derisively, and when Takoda freed him, Kovo bounded up the stairs ahead of the boy.

Kovo raced up the spiral far faster than Takoda had expected, considering his massive size. Takoda had heard of people who could access the strengths of their spirit animals. He tried to focus on his bond as he made his way up the tower, much more slowly than Kovo. But the climb didn't feel any faster than before.

When Takoda finally reached the top, Kovo was standing majestically on his four massive limbs, his back arched as he stared out over the horizon. He studied the distance, as if he was waiting for something or someone to appear.

"If you're watching for the sunrise, then you're looking in the wrong direction," Takoda told him. Kovo gave no response.

When the sun finally appeared, it was little more than a sliver of bright red light on the horizon, not yet lighting the full sky. When Takoda suddenly rang the bell, it startled Kovo. He spun around, his deep-set eyes wide with panic. Takoda stifled a laugh as the infamous ape scowled at him.

Then Kovo turned and continued watching out the far window of the bell tower as Takoda delivered a second and then a third toll.

On the way down, the boy asked Kovo once again about their bond.

"What powers will you give me?" he asked. Again he was ignored. It was as if they weren't bonded at all, and Takoda was nothing to Kovo but a pest. "Come on," he said. "Will I be stronger? Faster? Smarter?"

But all Takoda felt was annoying.

When Takoda saw Sudo later that morning, the older boy avoided his eye. Takoda wondered if it was possible that Sudo had learned his lesson from their fight. More likely, it was the four-hundred-pound gorilla following Takoda throughout the monastery.

Kovo sniffed the air loudly as they passed the bully, then blew out again quickly. The gorilla grimaced, as if he smelled something foul, looking up at Sudo's frown. A few of the monks laughed as Sudo backed away, blushing.

Walking on, Takoda was nearly certain he noticed a brief smile appear on Kovo's menacing face.

Before the midday chant, Ananda came to Takoda's room. She handed him a satchel with charcoal and a scroll of papyrus. The boy expected her to dole out additional punishment, asking him to transcribe monastery doctrine from memory, or to use it for something equally tedious. So he was surprised when she explained what the scroll was for.

"It's for Kovo," she said. "So he can draw in a more productive manner."

Ananda then handed Takoda a package. It was wrapped ceremoniously, as if it were a special gift.

Kovo watched suspiciously as Takoda unwrapped it. Inside, the boy found a new monastery robe. This one was blue, like Ananda's, instead of the warmer saffron. There wasn't a stain or tear to be found on the luxurious garment.

"You have a spirit animal now," she said. "You should dress accordingly."

"Should I change into it now?" Takoda asked her, unable to contain his excitement. "Is it okay if I wear it to meditation?"

"About that . . ." Ananda said. She sighed, taking the robe back from him. She folded it and packed it neatly into the satchel. Then the old monk glanced over Takoda's shoulder, toward the doorway.

There, standing in the midday sun, was a light-skinned boy with golden hair. He was about Takoda's height, but that seemed to Takoda to be the only thing the two of them had in common. At least, until a large wolf with cobalt blue eyes followed the boy into the room.

Upon seeing the two together, Takoda knew instantly who they were. He gaped at the heroic duo, then flushed when the boy nodded at him.

"Takoda, this is Conor," Ananda said. "I need you to trust him. He's here to take you and Kovo to a safer place."

Ananda must have known the words would hurt Takoda, because she said them with a great deal of compassion. Still, all Takoda could hear was that he was about to lose his home again. Along with the closest thing he had to a family. And what was Takoda to believe he was gaining, other than an infamously treacherous spirit animal who wanted nothing to do with him?

Kovo.

And that's what this was really about, wasn't it? The gorilla was perhaps the greatest villain in the history of Erdas. As a Great Beast he had nearly destroyed the world–twice. The Greencloaks would never let so dangerous a creature out of their sight again. That was what Ananda meant by taking them to a safer place–safer for the rest of the world.

What will they think of me? Takoda wondered. *The boy who summoned Kovo?*

In the stories Takoda had heard of the four heroes of Erdas, Conor was always described as the kind one. He was the gentle shepherd, forced by circumstance to be a hunter and leader. And yet the young Greencloak seemed to be wrestling with his anger as he gazed at Kovo chained to the wall.

Briggan didn't even try. The wolf growled openly at the ape, his hackles rising. Takoda remembered his father telling him that Kovo had killed Briggan himself, back when the two were both still Great Beasts.

The ape watched them both impassively, his brooding red eyes practically glowing in the sunlight. If he was surprised to see his former enemies, his face didn't show it.

"That's him all right," Conor said, taking a breath. He pushed his hand into Briggan's fur and the wolf calmed somewhat, his growl slowly fading.

A wave of despair fell over Takoda. The Greencloaks would hate *him*, too, just because he was bonded to Kovo. All of Erdas would hate him.

"Neither of you are safe here," Conor said, as if he knew something that they didn't. "There's someone out there hunting the Great Beasts." His blue eyes met Takoda's, and Takoda was surprised by what he saw there. Pity . . . and worry.

Only then did Takoda begin to believe what Ananda had told him. He was not safe. And neither was Kovo.

But what safer place could there have been than the isolated Niloan monastery, wedged between virgin forest and the mouth of a guarded river?

"Zerif knows where you are," Conor said nervously. "It's only a matter of time. We really need to hurry."

Zerif? Takoda was sure he'd heard the name before. Something about the war.

Takoda had nothing but questions for Conor. *Why me? Why has Kovo returned? Isn't the war over?* But Conor was already out the door, the gray wolf leading the way.

Kovo beat his chest, gibbering at Takoda urgently to unlock his chains from the wall. He *wanted* to go with the Greencloaks?

Takoda didn't feel ready. He glanced around his modest room. He had no belongings, other than the satchel in Ananda's hands. She rushed to unlock Kovo's chains, then stepped to Takoda and threw the satchel's leather strap over his head.

Takoda stared up into the monk's kind eyes, trying to think of what to say. But nothing came. Ananda hugged him tightly, not saying a word. The hug wasn't nearly long enough when Kovo interrupted, pulling Takoda roughly from Ananda and toward the doorway.

Takoda couldn't help but think of his mother's final embrace, and how the metal armor had hurt his chest. Ananda's hug hurt, too. Possibly worse, because this time Takoda knew it was a good-bye. Probably forever.

Kovo's muscular fist tugged him down the corridor. Takoda turned back to see the monk wiping tears from her eyes. When she saw him she smiled, holding up her bright palm.

"Now you get to run," Ananda called after Takoda.

And run they did.

Takoda chased Kovo down a long arcade, barely able to keep up with him. They turned, rushing down a brightly lit corridor, and then raced up a tall flight of stairs, a crowd of old monks and students leaping out of the way. Takoda thought he saw Sudo among them, but he was running too fast up the stairs to look back. When they reached the top, he spied Conor pointing toward something in the sky.

An eagle was circling high above the monastery. Takoda squinted to look, covering his eyes from the glare of the noon sun.

"It's Halawir!" Conor gasped. "Zerif is closer than I thought. We have to find a quicker way to the river."

Briggan leaped over the edge of the walkway, splashing into an elevated aqueduct below. Conor did the same, and Kovo and Takoda followed, jumping less elegantly into the cold channel of shallow water. They followed the flow, high above the cloisters and gardens of the monastery. Takoda carried his satchel above his head, the swift water tugging at his ankles and waist as Kovo tore off in front of him, water splashing in all directions.

Then, with as little warning as Takoda had been given before, Conor climbed over the channel's edge and jumped down. Takoda leaned to look, half expecting to see the boy's lush green cloak still falling through the air. Instead, he found Conor splashing into a second channel, only ten feet down at most.

"Maybe now's not the best time to tell you all this, but I can't swim very well," Takoda said between breaths. But none of them seemed to be listening.

Takoda paused, afraid to jump into the deeper water. Kovo reached for him. Or was he reaching for the satchel?

The ape thumped his back. It must have been just a gentle pat for the gorilla, but Takoda was sent sprawling forward into the water. A moment later, Kovo landed beside him with an enormous splash.

Together, the group waded through even more rapid water. Takoda hurried to keep up, but he was clumsy and out of his element. Eventually, they climbed out over a ledge, between two massive pillars that marked the entrance to the infirmary.

Briggan paused to shake water droplets from his silvery coat as the rest of them caught their breath. Huffing, Conor stared at the sky again.

Takoda looked up and saw Halawir circling closer, as if to signal the group's exact location. It cried out, the shrill sound echoing throughout the stone architecture of the monastery.

Conor started to lead them down another set of stairs, heading toward an open courtyard.

"No!" Takoda called after him. "This way!" He pointed toward the double doors of the infirmary. "There's a passage inside. No one will see us."

Takoda showed the group inside, where a staircase led past storerooms of medicinal herbs, and then all the way down to ground level. It was a massive shortcut, and Takoda felt briefly proud for having helped a hero like Conor find his way.

At the foot of the stairs, they sprinted down the row of granary cells. Water was still dripping off Takoda's robe, and he was careful not to slip on the stones. Behind him, Takoda heard Kovo's chains jangling as he knuckled along. They dashed through the granary exit, and eventually out through the mill.

Then it was Briggan's turn to lead again. He sniffed the outside air, choosing which direction would lead them toward the river. But as he rounded the base of the mill house, the wolf stopped in his tracks fifty feet or more from the edge of a stretch of farmland.

There was a rustling among the wheat crops, and with each passing moment the sound intensified. Out of the tall stalks a savage-looking boar appeared. Its white tusks flashed brightly as it leaped out of the shade and into the sunlight, charging toward the group.

Kovo rose onto his hind legs and beat his black chest with his fists, ready to attack. But Briggan barked at the gorilla and swiftly changed course, leading them away in the opposite direction.

"There will be others. Too many to fight," Conor rushed to explain. Then he followed the cue of his spirit animal, sprinting away.

Kovo stood down, but not without first baring his fangs at the approaching beast. The boar snorted, flaring its nostrils as it dashed toward them with alarming speed.

They fled uphill between the forest and the outer wall of the monastery. But the boar was gaining on them. Takoda ran as fast as he could, his robe clinging to his legs. The other three quickly outpaced him, and Takoda feared at any moment he would feel the boar's tusks stab and slice the back of his tired calves.

Takoda could only move so quickly without tripping over rocks. By the time he had caught up with the other three, they were sprinting along the perimeter of the monastery.

As soon as he lost sight of their enemy, Takoda wanted to rest. But the group rushed farther, up a rocky slope. It was steep, and soon none of them were running, but pulling themselves up boulder by boulder.

Briggan barked, and when Takoda looked up, he saw yet another foe had appeared.

A ram with huge curled horns reared back, high above them on the rocks. Bright sunlight glared from behind the animal, stinging Takoda's eyes. The ram bayed loudly. Then it, too, charged at the four. Its hooves clattered sharply as they hit the stones. For a moment Takoda stared in awe of the creature's speed, navigating the steep rocks as it barreled forward, lowering its horns. It was as if the ram was carrying the full force of the wind behind him as he raced down the rocks, ready to pummel them all with his bony skull.

Briggan and Conor leaped out of the way, off the rocks, followed by Kovo. But Takoda's sandals were slippery. As he rushed to push off the boulder he was climbing, he slid, twisting his ankle and then falling forward and skinning his knees with a crash.

Takoda looked up to see Kovo leaping back up into the ram's path. The gorilla leaned into the wind with his palms open, like a wrestler readying himself. The ram bayed again, charging at full speed. The shrill sound of the animal's battle cry multiplied as it echoed between the jagged rocks and the high monastery wall.

Takoda crouched, curling up between rocks. The boy knew the force of the ram was enough to send Kovo flying backward into him. Instead, the ape caught the ram by the horns, just before the moment of impact. Kovo twisted, redirecting the momentum of the massive animal and tossing him downhill, right over Takoda's head. The boy turned in time to see the ram tumble, his four hooves cutting into the soil right in front of the stumbling boar. Together the two rolled far down the slope.

Kovo stood tall on his hind legs, beating his chest. He roared loudly down at them, looming over Takoda.

When Kovo was finished, Takoda tried to stand, but he couldn't. Seeing him falter, the ape lifted Takoda from under his arms and carried him onto his back. Then he ambled into the forest with the others.

Takoda held on tight to Kovo's dark hair. Panic still quaked in his blood. His ears were ringing.

For a moment Takoda thought the questions he had about Kovo's loyalty were answered. He didn't have to save him, after all. And yet Kovo did, blocking him from harm with his own body. But then he remembered the satchel around his neck, and he wondered if it was the papyrus Kovo cared about instead. Or maybe the gorilla was simply itching for a fight, a creature of perpetual war.

Whatever Kovo's reasons, Takoda was grateful. He clung to the ape's back, hoping Kovo could feel it.

"This way," Conor yelled, and the three followed him, crashing through low branches along a steep creek. Takoda pushed his face into Kovo's fur as leaves scraped the back of his neck. Twigs caught on the strap of the satchel, snapping as they broke. But Takoda held on.

Before he knew it, Takoda could feel Kovo standing taller on his four limbs. Takoda felt the dappled sunshine hit his back, and then full sun. When he looked up, he saw the river. It gleamed blue and green, light twinkling at the far water's edge, where a boat waited at the end of a long dock.

"Kalani! Get the boat ready for launch!" Conor screamed. A Greencloak on the boat waved back to him, then hurried to untie the ropes. Takoda squinted, trying to make out what her spirit animal might be, but couldn't find any sign of one. Then he noticed a spray of mist from the water beside the boat, and realized a dolphin was swimming alongside it.

Conor and Briggan ran toward the dock, despite their exhaustion.

Kovo followed at first, but soon he was dashing forward at full speed. Takoda held on tightly as they gained on the others. Kovo raced toward the water as if his life depended on it. And perhaps it did. Perhaps all of theirs did.

Kovo passed Conor, Takoda riding on the ape's back. And then they passed Briggan, too, as they neared the dock.

But as Kovo approached it, a huge white bear crashed out of the water, blocking his way. Startled, Kovo jolted to the side, and Takoda lost his grip. The boy tumbled to the ground again, nearly rolling into the water. His satchel was thrown from his shoulder and onto the muddy ground.

The bear growled loudly. Then it stood on its hind legs, taller than even Kovo. It roared through open jaws, river water pouring onto the dock from its matted white fur. Then it let itself fall back to standing, its two front paws hitting the wood planks with a heavy bang.

Kovo roared ferociously, gnashing his teeth. Briggan snarled from behind the ape, still running toward the dock.

Kalani, the Greencloak on the boat, cried out for the group to hurry, a rope coiled tightly in her hands. Takoda could see that she was struggling to hold the boat in place against the river's current.

The white bear swatted a huge paw in Kovo's direction as the two faced off. Kovo burst forward suddenly, his enormous hand snatching a fistful of the polar bear's fur. But just as it looked like Kovo might win the upper hand, the bear disappeared into a flash of light.

"Children," Takoda heard a snide voice say. "Where do you think you're going?"

They all turned to see a bearded man walking toward them. His dark tunic was open at his chest, caught in a chilling breeze. There on his chest, stretching high onto the muscles of his shoulder, was the tattoo of the white bear. And across from it, an outstretched boar. The ram and eagle were partially visible as well.

Takoda wondered, *How many spirit animals can one person have? How many others are hidden under that tunic?*

But as frightening as the sight of all those tattoos might have been, it was the mark on the man's forehead that turned the boy's blood cold. The same bloody spiral from Kovo's drawings pulsed there, like a third eye.

"I don't know what you're planning, but you won't get away with it, Zerif," Conor said. The man ignored him.

As Zerif stepped toward them, a wicked smile stretched across his face. Kovo stumbled backward, nearly crushing the satchel. The ape picked it up and slung the leather strap around his own neck.

Takoda pushed himself to his feet. His ankle was tender, but it wasn't broken. *If we all make a run for the boat, will I make it?* he thought. *Or will they leave me behind?*

Zerif reached into his pocket and pulled out a small black bottle. Briggan growled from the dock as soon as he saw it. Takoda looked wildly from the boat to Conor, and from Briggan to Kovo. Every one of them stood frozen in anticipation as Zerif pulled out the cork stopper. But not Takoda.

"Run!" he screamed, not waiting to see what evil was about to be unleashed. He dashed as quickly as he could up the dock and toward the boat, with Kovo following his lead. Kalani passed him the taut rope. Then she drew a throwing spear from the floor, and before Takoda knew what was happening behind him, she drove it heavily toward Zerif.

Takoda turned to see if the spear had hit, but it was Conor who cried out in pain. He had accidentally run into the spear's path. He covered a wound on his wrist, pulling his arm to his chest.

"No!" Kalani cried.

Briggan knocked Zerif to the ground, but the man freed himself almost immediately. He grabbed the wolf by the scruff of his neck and managed to lift the massive animal off the ground as he stood.

"At last!" Zerif cackled, raising the bottle to Briggan's snout. Takoda watched as something small and dark twisted inside the glass.

All eyes were on the bottle as Conor threw himself into Zerif's side. Briggan fell to the ground, and so did the bottle. It bounced and rolled quickly toward the river. But before falling into the rushing water, something dark writhed out of it and onto the wet ground. It was a worm, or a slug. Takoda wasn't sure, but he watched it in horror. Whatever it was, it slithered in Briggan's direction with otherworldly speed. It moved like a shadow across the ground, twisting over rocks and bubbling across the surface of a mud puddle.

Briggan yelped and whined, tripping over the foot of the dock as he tried desperately to back away. Conor freed himself from Zerif's grip, pushing to his feet. He pulled out his ax and struck the worm, mere inches away from the wolf's paw. Then Conor stomped at the ground violently as Zerif stood, the same strange smile on his face.

Conor must have seen it, too, because he made a break for it, down the dock. He and Briggan leaped on board just as Takoda let go of the rope. Immediately, the boat jolted forward, downstream.

Kalani rushed to Conor, hurrying to care for the wound her spear had left at the boy's wrist. As Takoda watched, feeling helpless, he was startled by a slither of movement at his neck. It was only Kovo, returning the satchel. Still, he shuddered involuntarily, thinking of the strange worm on the dock.

"Thank you," Takoda said as the ape lowered the strap around the boy's neck.

Takoda and Kovo turned to watch Zerif as the boat hurried away. The boy expected him to send Halawir into the air after them, or perhaps there was some slithering sea serpent he'd let lose into the water with a flash.

Instead, the menacing man simply waved from the shore, the same unmistakable smirk on his face.

"What was that?" Takoda asked Kovo. But the ape didn't have an answer.

Just then, they heard Conor drop his ax.

When Takoda looked, he saw a severed half of the worm twisting up Conor's middle finger and the back of his hand. Conor tried desperately to shake the worm loose and into the water, but it was much too quick.

Before any of them knew what was happening, it wiggled into the wound at Conor's wrist, then disappeared. Conor clamped a hand down over the wrist, hissing between his teeth.

Takoda gasped, and Kalani's hands covered her mouth.

Conor's eyes were wide, staring down at his wrist. Whatever was happening beneath the skin, he covered it from view of the others.

"What was that thing?" Takoda asked. "What . . . what do we do?"

Conor seemed to come to. He pulled his wrist weakly to his chest, casting a glance at Takoda. There was so much in that look—fear, anger, disappointment. Takoda himself had felt those very same things the moment he summoned Kovo.

He's wondering if I'm worth it, Takoda realized bleakly.

"We have to get to Greenhaven," Conor said. His voice was tight with barely restrained emotion. "I have a feeling things are about to get worse."

GERATHON

BETRAYAL

By Brandon Mull

ROOTS AND VINES SNAGGED AT HER ANKLES AS RAISHA made her way along the uneven path between the ferny shrubs, a yoke across her shoulders, water buckets dangling at either end. Dense branches interlocked overhead, filtering the sun's rays into a greenish twilight. The steamy air tasted of damp leaves. Perspiration greased her skin.

She tromped forward, the muscles in her legs burning, her sense of balance faltering. High above, monkeys shrieked and tropical birds squawked. Who knew what else prowled unseen in the underbrush? The jungles of southern Zhong housed many predators, including tigers, leopards, and giant constrictors.

Would it be so bad to become a meal for a tiger? What if a venomous snake struck her?

No. The guards wouldn't allow it. Death would be a form of escape. They'd find a way to intervene. If a giant constrictor swallowed her, who would haul water from the outpost? Urban's precious mule might have to pitch in.

Somewhere up ahead, concealed by trees and foliage, loomed the Mire, a Greencloak prison built on an island of muck in the midst of a tropical swamp. Dripping cells, mossy yards, and leaning towers combined to form a hideous abomination of iron, stone, and mildew—the entire complex slowly sinking into the bog.

Raisha had first arrived with escape on her mind. But tight security, high walls, and the surrounding wetlands soon showed her why the Greencloaks had transferred her there. Prisoners did not escape from the Mire. The other inmates seemed resigned to their fate.

Multiple wells inside the prison offered fresh water, but the prison's warden insisted that those in her custody haul their own water from the nearest Greencloak outpost in order to get exercise. Raisha suspected the real reason was to exhaust and dishearten the inmates by working them like slaves. But the chore did provide certain opportunities. . . .

"Pick up the pace," Urban called over his shoulder. A pudgy man astride a mule, the Greencloak's dark eyes glared at her from beneath a sloppy crown of knotted rags.

Grunting, Raisha walked faster. Every other day since arriving at this awful place, she had followed

Urban on his mule from the outpost, watching the animal's furry haunches rock from side to side as it plodded along.

But today things were a bit different. Today she had poured extra water into her buckets—twice the normal load. Working hard was part of her plan.

"I'm twelve," she reminded Urban.

"Old enough to commit adult crimes and get sent to a very adult prison," Urban said. "Only criminals designated as threats to all of Erdas join us here in the tropics."

"I was used," Raisha insisted.

"You helped to separate people from their spirit animals," Urban accused. "Is any crime more despicable?"

"It's a favor if your spirit animal is a mule," Raisha said, panting.

"Brave words from somebody without an animal companion," Urban scoffed. "Good thing you don't have one. The poor creature would have little freedom."

Raisha still harbored a hope that she might summon an animal one day. But no way was she going to share that with this annoying guard. "Isn't your mule just as trapped as my animal would be?"

Urban gave a derisive laugh. "Lucky loves the jungle, don't you, boy?" He patted the mule. "We're only at the Mire part of each day. And our assignment here will end in a year or so. What are your prospects? Thirty years, minimum, if I remember."

"Yes," Raisha said, lowering her eyes.

The Greencloak rode in silence for a few blessed

moments. "Come now," Urban said finally, his voice softening a touch. "You have to accept what you did. You were caught and now you're here. It's reality–but this doesn't have to be the end for you. Take responsibility for your crimes. Shape up. You can still make something of yourself."

Raisha would have scoffed if she weren't running out of breath. Who was this guy to talk? Some backwoods turnkey on a shabby mule. She didn't want or need encouragement from her captors.

Bowing her head, she concentrated on walking. She'd made this trek several times now, and it was never easy, but the extra water she had added was making it impossible. Her legs were rubbery, and her balance was becoming untrustworthy. She staggered, sloshing water from the buckets.

Urban snapped at the convict ahead of him. Raisha wondered if she might actually faint. The plan was to become so exhausted that when she faked passing out, it would look real enough to fool her jailor. If she actually lost consciousness, she could miss her chance to make an escape. And if she kept pushing, truly fainting was possible.

Who needed to scale walls if the guards took you on a walk through the jungle every other day? A chain was only as strong as the weakest link, and a prison wall only served if you remained inside.

Raisha needed to make her move soon, before they reached the marshier part of the jungle around the Mire. She was willing to risk running through dense vegetation, whether or not hidden predators lurked among the fronds and reeds—but the gloomy waters of the swamp were too forbidding.

A root decided the matter. Raisha tripped, dropping the yoke. Buckets clattered and water splashed. She stayed down, her cheek on the firm, warm mud of the trail. The ground seemed to gently teeter.

"On your feet!" Urban barked.

He sounded distant. Oh no. Maybe she really *would* fade off to sleep.

"Give me a break," he grumbled. Raisha heard his boots slap the mud as he dismounted. She heard him tromp over to her. Her breathing was labored. She tried to keep it regular.

A boot slid under her ribs and flipped her onto her back. Now was the crucial moment. She did her best to stay limp. A chance for escape depended on it.

"What's the holdup?" a guard asked from behind where Raisha had fallen.

"On your feet," Urban demanded again. Raisha gave no reaction and let the pause stretch out.

"She's playing possum," said the guard from behind.

Raisha felt a finger slide into her nostril. Fear, will, and sheer exhaustion helped her resist flinching. The finger poked inside her ear. There came a pause. Then a hand slapped her cheek hard enough to sting. She kept her body slack.

"She might really be out," Urban said, a touch of concern in his voice.

"Drag her to the side," the other guard suggested. "Let us pass. Then tie her up and throw her on Lucky."

"Will do," Urban replied.

Strong hands seized her ankles and Raisha felt herself sliding through mud, out of the way. Then she heard other inmates and guards passing.

If she waited until she was tied up, Raisha knew she would have no chance to escape. Timing would be everything.

As she heard the last of the procession passing, she opened her eyes a crack. Urban stood beside his stinky mule, uncoiling a length of rope.

"Don't turn your back on her," the last guard cautioned. "Want me to stay around?"

"Go on ahead," Urban said. "I won't be far behind. If I can't handle a young girl, what use am I?"

A fair question, Raisha thought.

"She's no ordinary young girl," the other guard warned.

"She committed unordinary crimes," Urban said. "But she's nothing extraordinary."

The dismissive comment made Raisha's cheeks burn beneath the streaks of mud. The problem was, he had a point. She hadn't accomplished her missions through abnormal strength or speed or agility. As an unassuming girl without a spirit animal, the daughter of a prosperous merchant, she had used her normalcy to her advantage. She could go places many people couldn't go without being questioned. If she got caught somewhere she shouldn't be, she could pretend she had lost her way. Who was going to arrest a respectable young girl who seemed accidentally lost—or perhaps had gotten a little curious?

But now she had been unmasked. Anonymity no longer protected her. She couldn't make excuses or invoke the name of her father to dodge trouble.

And there was no way she was going to overpower a Greencloak guard, even slovenly Urban.

But she might be able to run from him.

If she got a head start and raced wildly, taking risks he was unwilling to take, maybe she could create some distance and slip away. The dense jungle held perils, but nothing so fearsome as thirty years in a sinking cage.

The last Greencloak guard in the procession passed out of view around a bend in the trail. Urban still stood beside his mule, cutting the rope. He was only seven or eight paces from Raisha, but the guard would never be farther away or more distracted before coming to bind her.

Wishing she felt a little less exhausted, Raisha rolled over and pushed herself quickly to her feet. She charged into the lush undergrowth. Broad fronds parted in a series of limp slaps. Pliable branches yielded to her legs. She weaved around trunks and plunged through shrubs.

"Raisha, no!" Urban called. "Don't be a fool!"

She heard him crash into the undergrowth behind her, prompting a frantic surge of speed. Heart hammering, she shot forward, hurdling a fallen log shaggy with moss.

Without the buckets, her body felt light. She might be small, but she was quick, and Urban's bulky size would hinder him in the dense foliage. She darted through a stand of bamboo, making the cluster of poles clack and rattle. Raisha cursed between heaving breaths. The noise would signal her exact location to anyone with half a brain.

"Raisha!" Urban yelled, revealing that she had already gained a little ground on him. "Halt! Come back before you get hurt!"

Raisha's mind raced almost as fast as her heart. No way would she get duped by his desperate bluff. If she got away, yes, she would be lost in the jungle. And that involved a host of dangers. But if she headed northeast, she would eventually reach Xin Kao Dai and the surrounding villages. The reward was worth the hazards.

Blinking hard, Raisha fought off a bout of light-headedness. Her body really had been exhausted. Wouldn't that be perfect if she passed out now? No! She might never get another chance like this.

Gritting her teeth, Raisha charged ahead through a curtain of vines.

And suddenly she was on the ground, arms pinned against her torso, legs lashed together. The vines had collapsed around her like a dozen constrictors. No. It was netting—a trap concealed in the vines.

Raisha bucked and squirmed, but the net only embraced her tighter. Her head ached and the ground seemed to rock beneath her. She stopped struggling and lay on her back, hot and sweaty, staring up at layers of leafy limbs that blocked out all but the tiniest glimpses of blue sky, minuscule windows of freedom.

"Are you all right?" Urban called, not too far off now.

"I'm not dead," Raisha responded mirthlessly.

"Then you're fortunate," Urban said. She could hear him bulling his way through the foliage as he drew nearer. "We've been using this trail for decades. There are traps all over the place. And before long, you would have reached waterways that connect to the swamp. Did you honestly think running was an option?"

Raisha didn't answer. Why wouldn't a hungry tiger just come eat her?

Then the furry head of a mule entered her field of vision. Showing its teeth, the animal brayed in a way that Raisha could only conclude was laughter.

Indirect sunlight filtered into the cell through a long shaft in the ceiling too narrow for her to enter. A rusty grate protected the mouth of the shaft, and iron bars crisscrossed beyond at intervals. By the weak light, Raisha watched water rippling down one wall and across the floor to a congested drain.

This was her third day in solitary confinement in one of the wet cells. The volume of water on the ground varied, but was seldom less than an inch, or more than three. The prisoners whispered that the entire floor of this wing would eventually sink into the bog, as the floor below it had done years ago.

Upon her arrival in solitary, Raisha had been told by her jailors that there would be no more fresh water coming, so her best chance for a semi-sanitary drink was to lick it off the walls. After several hours scantly slurping water that tasted of minerals and mildew, some guards brought her a pitcher of water and a hunk of stale bread. Their laughter still echoed in her mind.

Raisha huddled on her cot–the one place in her cell where she could keep dry. For the millionth time, she cursed herself for getting caught. Everything had been going so well! Her life had been an adventure! Working for Zerif had been a glorious, empowering game. Before Zerif entered her life, Raisha had always felt ignored. Her father doted on her brothers. Her mother obsessed about their place in society. Raisha had no real companionship, and no real destiny. But she had used the invisibility that comes with being ignored to accomplish amazing things.

The days alone in the wet cell had helped confirm the reality that her life had permanently changed. Her dash into the jungle now seemed childish and stupid. There would be no escape. Life as she had known it was over.

Raisha shook with sobs. She should have been more careful! Zerif should have rescued her before she got here. Was there any chance he would come for her now?

No. With her cover blown, she would be of little use to him. The dealings and travels of her father had granted her access that Zerif found useful. Raisha would learn a dignitary's schedule, or leave a door unlocked, or deliver a package, and consequently earn praise and gifts from the future ruler of Erdas. And then there were the Great Beasts! Creatures of legend, taken as easily as if they'd been dogs in the street.

If she could go back, would she do it differently? How could she have resisted the thrill? Her involvement with Zerif had been the secret spice in her life, making everything else mean more. Without that secret, who would she have been? Nobody. Another silly merchant-class girl who pretended to have interests until she was married off to some insipid merchant-class boy. She would never have done anything important, and there would have been no adventure in her life.

Looking around her tomblike cell, Raisha breathed in the damp air. Was this what adventure looked like? Rotting in a half-drowned tomb? The thought of being here a week more was too much. Let alone a year. Or ten. Or thirty.

Raisha felt crushed by the weight of all those years piled on top of her. Hauling water through the jungle. Huddling in a humid cell eating tasteless goo. This wasn't living.

Leaning back on the cot, Raisha laced her fingers behind her head. She wished she could sleep for the next thirty years. It would be better than the uncomfortable monotony that awaited. She would surely lose her mind.

No—after her escape attempt, it might be *more* than thirty years. If the Greencloaks felt she was such a threat, did she have any guarantee they would ever release her?

It was going to be a long, slow, wretched life.

The light from the window shaft dimmed. Had a cloud swiftly overtaken the sun? And was there less torchlight coming in from the corridor? Were the torches burning out? In the dimness, rats started squeaking in the walls. Raisha sat up, the hairs on her neck standing upright. She hated the rats at the Mire. They were too big.

Raisha felt an odd tingling. The entire prison began to tremble, stones groaning. The water on the floor of her cell sloshed. Then came a searing flash and a crash like thunder.

As Raisha blinked away the afterimage of the brilliant light, her eyes fell to a motion on the floor of her cell. The light from the shaft into her room was back to normal, and she could see a snake flowing toward her in looping curves, long body undulating like a ribbon in a river.

With a scream stuck in her throat, Raisha scooted to the opposite side of her cot from the serpent. The rats had grown quiet, but this was much worse!

The snake reared up, revealing a yellow underside in contrast to the black scales elsewhere. A hood spread out, framing the head. The cobra swayed gently, and a thin tongue flicked out.

As Raisha gazed at the cobra, she began to collect her thoughts. She was still tingling and felt inexplicably drawn to the snake. The temporary dimness, the upheaval of the prison, the squeaking rats, and the flash of light began to add up in her mind. Had she just summoned a spirit animal? Here? Now?

Chills tingled through her as the serpent edged nearer, holding its head above the edge of the cot. Raisha studied the cobra as it swayed hypnotically. Black eyes rimmed in gold returned her gaze.

Raisha slowly reached a hand toward the snake. If the animal struck her, the bite could be fatal. Yet she felt strangely calm, her fingers drawn toward the reptile almost against her will.

The cobra stopped swaying. The stillness made her hesitate inches from contact, then her fingertips brushed the side of its hood, and Raisha gasped at the spark that reverberated through her body. The invigorating jolt was accompanied by a sense of relief, as if she were finally breathing after a long pause.

For a moment, Raisha sensed people throughout the prison in varied states of alarm, mostly in rooms and yards above her present position. Thoughts and conversations about the recent quaking came to her in jumbled snippets. She could taste the odor of her cell.

"You're Gerathon," Raisha said in amazement.

The cobra dipped her head in acknowledgment, then bared slender fangs in a reptilian parody of a smile.

"I'm Raisha," she said breathlessly. Tears blurred her vision. She had always hoped to call a spirit animal, and had also felt a quiet certainty that it wouldn't happen. Nobody in her family had summoned one for generations. But now, in her hour of need, here was one of the most powerful animals of all time. The mighty Gerathon!

The cobra dipped her head again.

From beyond the door of her cell, Raisha heard voices and the clinking of keys. The sounds snapped her out of her trance.

"You need to hide!" Raisha warned Gerathon. "We're in a Greencloak prison. The Mire. I don't know what they'll do if they find you here."

The voices drew nearer.

In spite of her fear of discovery, Raisha couldn't resist grinning. "You used to be bigger, right? That's not an insult. You're a full-sized cobra, but you used to be gigantic. You're still too large to hide in here. But not too big to fit up the shaft to my pathetic window."

Raisha leaped to her feet, splashing as she dragged the cot beneath the window shaft. Picking up the sleek cobra, Raisha found her heavy and awkward to hold. But she climbed onto the cot and managed to lift the sinuous reptile above her head.

Hood down, Gerathon squirmed through the grate and up into the shaft. Keys rattled in the cell door. Just as the cobra's tail disappeared through the grate, the door opened.

Payu, a tall, stern-eyed female guard, stepped down into the room, her boots plopping into the water. "What are you doing?"

Raisha kept her eyes away from the shaft. She could feel the guilt on her face, and she knew that standing on her cot looked suspicious. Would the guard notice she was right below the shaft?

"I heard rats in the walls," Raisha said. "They were going crazy."

Urban entered the room behind Payu. "So you climbed onto your cot?" he asked.

"I didn't know if the rats were going to flood into my cell," Raisha said. "I was freaked out."

"You moved the cot," Payu noted.

"Under the light port," Urban added, sloshing across the room. Leaning over the cot, he peered up the shaft.

Raisha looked up as he did. There was no sign of the cobra.

"I thought maybe the light would scare the rats," Raisha said.

Stepping back, Urban folded his arms. "This smells fishy."

"It's mildew," Raisha corrected.

"I saw the lights dim, Raisha," Urban went on. "I know what it looks and sounds like when a spirit animal is summoned. We all do. Only three of the prisoners here are of the proper age to summon a spirit animal, yourself included. Our guards are checking on the other two."

"You're a criminal," Payu said. "But summoning a spirit animal is no crime. We wouldn't punish a newly called animal for your past mistakes."

Unless the animal has committed crimes too, Raisha thought. *Like almost destroying Erdas in a former life.* "You think I called a spirit animal?" she asked sweetly.

Urban gave her a searching gaze. "Have it your way. We'll check up on the other possible candidates. But if you happened to summon a spirit animal, you don't need to hide it."

"Would you promise to be as good to my animal as you've been to me?" Raisha asked with mock sincerity.

Urban gave an incredulous chuckle. "Are you honestly complaining? You conspired to part people from their spirit animals, and you think prison is harsh? Plenty of people would have wanted you to hang for that crime. Raisha, you still have a chance here. Let us help you."

"Don't take her bait," Payu said.

"She's a kid," he replied.

Payu shook her head. "She looks like a child, but no true child would do what she did. That's why she's here. Come on. We'll check back later."

After Payu exited, Urban lingered in the doorway, staring. Was his look meant to convey sympathy? Did he want her to trust him? Was he out of his mind?

Raisha could hear Payu walking away, but Urban stepped back into the room. "I get that you hate it here. I know you see us as monsters for locking you up. But we're trying to protect the world from monsters like Zerif. You don't owe him your loyalty anymore. We both know he was using you."

Raisha looked away from Urban.

"We also both know you're no ordinary kid. You're special, Raisha. What kind of twelve-year-old can get into the kind of trouble you stirred up? And I'd bet my life savings that you called a spirit animal on top of it. Work with us. These walls won't only keep you in. They can keep Zerif out. We don't just want to save everyone else from him. We can also help save you."

Raisha wavered. Did she want to spend the next thirty years alone? Was it possible to form friendships with her Greencloak captors? Maybe even learn from them? No—those thoughts were pathetic. Urban just wanted to win her over so he could get info about Zerif. If he knew she had called Gerathon, he and every other Greencloak in Erdas would only want to control her.

She let her eyes return to his, a sneer curling her lip. "The last thing I need is the help of some joke who lives in a swamp with his mule."

Urban held her gaze for a long moment. She didn't see hurt there, and that made her feel a little awkward for being so harsh.

"At least I didn't steal my spirit animal," Urban said gently. "Nor would I want to steal yours." He stepped out and closed the door.

Raisha sat back down on her cot. The panic of danger, the thrill of summoning a beast of legend, and the fear of discovery had combined to leave her drained.

Leaning back, Raisha stared up the empty shaft. Where had Gerathon gone? Would the cobra return soon? Or would she abandon Raisha for a more comfortable life elsewhere? Could spirit animals do that?

Her thoughts turned to Zerif. He wanted to collect the Great Beasts. Where would his journeys take him next?

She abruptly sat up. Zerif was collecting Great Beasts. He had ways of figuring out where they would show up. Did that mean he would come for Raisha now? Was she important again?

Would he try to steal Gerathon? No, there was no need. Raisha had served him well. She would still serve him. Why separate her from the snake?

But would he see it that way?

Her heart rate sped up. Raisha couldn't be sure of anything. If Zerif did want to take Gerathon from her, was there any way to stop him? Not alone. But with Gerathon at her side, who knew what she might accomplish. It would be Raisha and her spirit animal against the world. Those odds might not be too terrible. After all, Gerathon had almost taken over the world once before.

But to have any chance, Raisha knew she absolutely had to escape.

That night, Raisha awoke with a hand covering her mouth. She reflexively struggled and tried to cry out.

"Not a word," a voice breathed in her ear. "I'm here to help."

Raisha forced herself to keep still. By the voice and hand she could tell that the figure looming over her was a man. A Greencloak? It wasn't Urban.

Raisha nodded and the hand slid away from her mouth. "Who are you?" she whispered.

"I'm Dorell," the voice replied. "I work in the kitchens here. But my loyalties lie elsewhere."

"Where do they lie?"

He didn't respond immediately. Raisha heard water trickling in the darkness. "Many believe a rumor that you summoned a spirit animal and are keeping it hidden. Is this so?"

"I don't know you," Raisha said.

"I serve one who you also served," Dorell replied. "One who believes you may have called an animal of great significance. If so, it won't be long before the Greencloaks discover this as well."

Raisha was fully aware that this stranger in her cell could be lying. He could be a Greencloak trying to trick the information out of her. He could also be working for Zerif, or he could be working for himself.

"Sorry to disappoint you," Raisha whispered. She gave a little shrug. "I didn't summon anything. Now get out of here before I scream."

"Decide very carefully," the stranger warned. "I'm prepared to extract you tonight. If you trust your captors more than me, so be it."

"You can get me out of here?" Raisha asked.

"The kitchens resupply with boats from the mainland," Dorell said. "I have a small craft standing ready."

Paralyzed by indecision, Raisha weighed her options. Were the Greencloaks more dangerous to her, or was Zerif? Urban was right that the prison walls offered some protection from her former employer. Would the Greencloaks try to separate her from Gerathon? Probably not. But they would most likely hold both of them prisoner for the rest of their lives.

What about Dorell? Was that even his real name? He could be anyone. Did he really work for Zerif? If so, it proved Zerif could get to her, even in the Mire. Dorell's mission *could* be to steal Gerathon. If not, his own agenda might not be any better.

Something plopped down beside Raisha, landing softly on her mattress. A muscular, scaly rope flexed against her arm, and she heard a fierce hiss.

Dorell released Raisha, sloshing through the water as he stepped back. He lit a lamp, revealing that he was a short man with lean features and large dark eyes. He looked much too scrawny to be lugging food around all day. His eyes widened as they fixed on the snake. "It's true," Dorell whispered. "You summoned *Her*."

Gerathon swiveled to gaze at Raisha, then slithered off the cot, landing on the floor with a splash. The cobra crossed to Dorell and claimed a position near his feet. Dorell kept still. The cobra looked at Raisha and hissed.

It seemed like Gerathon wanted to go. That was good enough for Raisha, who felt no path was clearly better than the others. At least she would get to leave with her spirit animal.

"If Gerathon trusts you, I'm sold," Raisha said.

"Fine," Dorell said. He extinguished the lamp. "Stay close."

Raisha stood up, submerging her feet in lukewarm water. In the dark, Dorell took her hand. He led her to the door and out of the cell.

An unseen lamp around a bend shed a little light in the mossy corridor. Like in her cell, water wept down the walls here, though the floor in the hall had better drainage.

"They did us a favor moving you to solitary," Dorell whispered. "This wing connects to a subcellar beneath the kitchens. Smuggling you out will be no trickier than sneaking a roll from the storeroom."

Dorell released her hand and led the way. Gerathon glided alongside her. As the corridor grew darker, Dorell glanced back, his eyebrows raised.

"After this corner there are no more lanterns, and we'll have to wade a bit," he whispered. "Small price for freedom, am I right?"

"Just go," Raisha said.

It soon became perfectly dark. They picked their way forward carefully through unseen debris, only an occasional drip or gurgle interrupting the silence. After scooting through a low gap in a wall, Raisha descended some steps into deeper water that came to her waist.

Raisha tried not to imagine what else might be lurking in these obscure waters. She did her best to stay beside Dorell.

"Gerathon is welcome to ride me," Dorell said. A moment later, he let out a nervous squeak. *"Ah! Excellent. I . . . feel her under my shirt. This will be an honor."*

Stretching out her hand, Raisha felt her cobra coiling around her guide's shoulders. The submerged ground remained uneven, so she stepped carefully. Below the water, Raisha's leg brushed against a greasy mass. Biting her lip to contain a shriek, Raisha floundered away from the contact. Dorell helped steady her.

"Are you all right?" he whispered.

"Let's just get out of here," Raisha muttered.

Still in blackness, they reached a wall of corroded bars. One had been removed, allowing Dorell and Raisha to slip through, though anybody much bigger would have had trouble.

"It gets deeper here," Dorell whispered.

Raisha took a step and nearly screamed. Suddenly she found herself immersed up to her neck, treading water. "This is more than wading," she hissed.

"Not far now," Dorell promised. "A short swim."

As she swam in the darkness, Raisha felt a slick shape ripple against her elbow. She shuddered but kept moving. The only way out of this was forward.

Before long they found a flight of stone stairs. Dorell led the way up and through a trapdoor. Lamplight reached them from an adjoining room.

"This is kept locked," Dorell murmured. "Good thing I'm trusted with the keys to the kitchens."

"No offense, but you could use some better cooks," Raisha said, wringing water from her sodden prison rags.

Dorell grinned. "You mean the slop they feed the prisoners? Not much effort wasted there. But the Greencloaks stationed here eat quite well. We should hurry."

With Gerathon still coiled around his neck and shoulders, Dorell hustled from one room to another until they reached a long corridor followed by a narrow stairway.

Peering down, Raisha saw that it descended to an iron door.

"Would you believe this will take us beyond the walls?" Dorell wagged his eyebrows conspiratorially.

"Really?" Raisha asked.

"The dock nearby is used to bring food in," Dorell said. "I already took care of the guard outside. And of course I have the key."

Raisha asked for no elaboration about the guard. She assumed Dorell had killed him and dumped the body in the swamp.

Dorell opened the door, and suddenly Raisha was following him along a tidy path under a starry sky and slim crescent moon. The walls of the Mire rose behind her. As usual, the night was warm. Not sweltering like in the day, but even with her clothes soaked, Raisha felt no chill.

They reached a little dock where a small skiff was tied up. "Not many boats," Raisha said.

"I sank three bigger ones," Dorell explained.

"You were that sure I'd come with you?" Raisha asked.

"My orders were clear," Dorell said. "Our master would have accepted nothing less. The Greencloaks won't know you're gone for hours. When they get wise, they'll have a hard time following us."

"I like how you think," Raisha said.

"I like being alive," Dorell replied. He held her hand as she boarded the skiff, then untied the craft and hopped in. He snatched up a pole and pushed them away from the dock.

By the scant moonlight, Raisha could see the prison tilting into the bog like some vast leviathan drowning in quicksand. She wondered how many years before the high walls would become part of the foundation.

As she got settled, Raisha noticed a pair of paddles in the bottom of the boat. "Want me to help?" she asked quietly.

"The pole will suffice," Dorell said. "We only row in emergencies. The route we'll take should avoid deep places."

"Where are we going?"

"To the biggest town we can reach by water. Wan Digal."

"How long will it take?"

Dorell shrugged, taking hold of the snake. "We should arrive before sunrise." With the pole in one hand, he tried to lift Gerathon off his shoulders, but the cobra wrapped tighter.

"I don't think she wants to get down," Raisha said with mock sweetness.

A flicker of fear passed through the man's eyes. "Wants to keep me in easy striking distance, does she?" Dorell asked. "Go ahead and kill me. See how far you two get in the swamp alone at night. No? Then get down."

The cobra loosed her hold of him and dropped to the bottom of the skiff. She glided over to Raisha and curled up in her lap like a coil of rope. Raisha stroked the sleek scales with two fingers.

"What happens in Wan Digal?" Raisha asked.

"We take steps to get you to Xin Kao Dai. Our master will be excited to greet you."

Raisha watched him pole them along. Dorell obviously knew the swamp well and handled the skiff with competence. She assumed that part of his job entailed making supply runs.

Would he have allies waiting in Wan Digal? How much should she trust him? Gerathon hadn't wanted to give up the position where she could strike him. That suggested the cobra didn't put much faith in him. Raisha wondered if Gerathon could still use her venom to control people, like the stories of the Great Serpent had said.

As shadowy trees and muddy islands drifted by, Raisha listened for the sounds of pursuit. How long before the Greencloaks realized she was missing? Surely they had other boats besides the ones Dorell had sabotaged. Some had spirit animals that could fly. Were they already coming for her?

How would Urban feel when he found her missing? She could picture him staring into her empty cell. The imagined bafflement gave her satisfaction, but it was surprisingly tinged with sadness. Could he have really seen something special in her? Did he sincerely want to help and protect her? Was she trading a safe haven for greater dangers?

Shaking her head, she scolded herself. *Right. Who would dare come after me with a mule standing guard?*

Freedom beat incarceration any day.

The moon blinked in and out of view between overhanging branches. Watching the sky, Raisha remembered her attempted escape just three days ago. It hadn't taken her very long to turn that around. She smiled and closed her eyes. Whatever happened now, at least she was free.

With nothing better to do, Raisha dozed. When she awoke, the moon was out of the sky, and the horizon was turning gray in one direction, making the stars fade.

"We're close to Wan Digal," Dorell said. "Clean getaway."

Raisha looked around. "You're sure the Greencloaks aren't after us?"

"If so, they're well behind us," Dorell said.

Raisha frowned. How could he be so confident without help? "You have a spirit animal," she said finally.

"Maybe," Dorell said with a grin. He gave no details, and Raisha didn't ask.

The predawn light increased. Before long, docks came into view up ahead. This deep in the jungle, Raisha had expected a fairly primitive village, but Wan Digal looked like an actual town. Smaller rowboats, canoes, rafts, and skiffs were attached to lesser quays, but several larger vessels were moored to bigger docks. Despite the early hour, there was already activity on the docks and some vessels out on the water.

When the skiff bumped against the quay, Gerathon attacked.

Dorell was ready. He leaped away just as the serpent lunged silently forward, kicking at the cobra. Gerathon struck his boot twice, then Raisha heard a shriek as a speckled brown and white bird—a marsh harrier—dove at the boat, talons outstretched.

Raisha grabbed a paddle from the bottom of the skiff. While Dorell stomped at Gerathon, she swung the paddle like a battle ax, whacking him on the back of the head. Dorell stumbled to his knees, and Gerathon sprang at him, striking madly.

The harrier stayed close, defending Dorell. Raisha took a swing at the bird of prey. She missed the harrier but struck Dorell on the ear. Gerathon got hold of the harrier with her jaws and promptly wrapped the bird in her coils. The harrier fell to the skiff's bottom like a stone. Feathers ruffled, it lurched and struggled against the serpent. Gerathon struck the bird once, twice, three times, her fangs dripping.

Then, slowly, the bird went limp.

Slumped on his back, Dorell stared at his fallen spirit animal, his breathing shallow, his face haggard. "Why?" he asked.

"I trust the cobra," Raisha said.

Dorell gave a sad smile. "You won't get far. Zerif . . . won't be pleased."

Gerathon hissed, and Raisha realized the snake was already on the quay. Raisha jumped out of the skiff without a look back and picked up the cobra, looping the snake over her shoulders. She walked toward the shore but immediately noticed a few fishermen moving toward her, waving their arms.

Raisha ran.

The fishermen ran too, boots clomping against the planks of the dock.

She made it to the buildings by the docks but wasn't far ahead of the oncoming fishermen. Raisha darted down an alley between two of the buildings. What if she got cornered? How many people could Gerathon take out?

"What do I do?" Raisha asked.

The cobra gave no answer.

Raisha ran hard. She wouldn't get caught now. They were almost free!

At the end of the alley, the world suddenly went dark.

Raisha screamed as an unseen assailant yanked a large canvas bag over her head and shoulders. It covered her down past her waist. Gerathon thrashed and hissed, trapped in the bag with her. Raisha struggled too, but strong arms held the bag in place, and a sharp chemical smell was making her woozy.

She couldn't pass out! She had to fight it! She had to get away! But her head was spinning, and it was becoming hard to move. Within moments she slipped into unconsciousness.

The dull ache in her head was her first sensation as Raisha awoke.

She tried to raise a hand to rub her skull but realized her arms were bound at her sides.

The discovery jerked her awake. She was in a small, dim room, strapped to a bed with a thin mattress. Raisha heaved and pulled, but her bindings held firm.

"There you are," spoke a rich, familiar voice from her past. "Don't waste energy struggling. Relax. Let's talk."

The voice filled her with a sickly mixture of excitement and dread.

Turning her head, Raisha locked eyes with Zerif, taking in his dark tunic and his neatly sculpted facial hair. He had caught her, but he apparently wanted words with her. Did that mean they might still be able to work together?

"You came," she said, hoping to sound like a lost little girl full of relief.

"I did," Zerif said with a bland smile. "You're happy to see me?"

"I thought you'd forgotten about me," Raisha replied.

"You can drop the act. You and Gerathon killed Dorell and his spirit animal."

"I'd never seen him before." Raisha maintained all the innocence she could muster. "I didn't know if he was being honest. When Gerathon attacked, I trusted her instincts."

"Her instincts weren't wrong," Zerif said. "Though Dorell did work for me."

"*I* work for you," Raisha blurted. "It can be like before. Wasn't I loyal? Gerathon and I will serve you well."

"Thank you for your past service," Zerif said, eyes glittering. "I appreciate the offer. You will indeed serve me. But wherever possible, I prefer a sure bet. This will leave no room for error." He held out a gloved hand. A small gray worm twisted on his palm.

"No, Zerif," Raisha pleaded, the words catching in her throat. She flinched away from the worm as much as the restraints would allow.

"Relax," Zerif said calmly. "Soon you'll have no cares at all."

"No!" Raisha shrieked. "This isn't right! I *called* her. Gerathon! *Gerathon, where are you?*"

Zerif nodded. "I knew you had the potential to summon a Great Beast." He brought a finger gently to his forehead, where a spiral looped beneath the skin. "Just as I knew where the others would awaken. That potential was part of why I worked with you. Inconvenient that it happened while you were imprisoned, but once again you proved *very* useful in smuggling yourself out. You helped others experience this fate, Raisha. Now it's your turn."

Crying hysterically, Raisha lunged against her restraints. She had dreamed of calling a spirit animal her whole life. It had happened more spectacularly than she could have guessed—summoning one of the Great Beasts. And yet she'd had less than a day with her new companion.

"Settle down," Zerif scolded, his hand coming toward her.

Raisha screamed frantically. What could she say to get out of this? What could she do? There was no time to think!

Zerif placed his palm on her forehead. "In a few moments your concerns will be forgotten. You will know the peace of a wholehearted purpose."

The worm wriggled just above her eyes. Tears streaming, Raisha whipped her head around, trying to shake it off. She strained against her bindings in vain. The worm broke through her skin and started burrowing. Worse than the physical pain was the horror of knowing what was to come.

She heard hissing from a corner of the room. Craning her neck, she could barely see where a basket was shaking. Gerathon was trying to get free!

"I'm sorry!" Raisha called to the cobra.

"Don't be," Zerif said. "I'll use her much more effectively than you would have. You'll both still serve the same master."

Raisha sobbed. How had she ended up in this nightmare? Was this what she had been doing to people? Faces flashed through her mind.

The hopeful, seafaring Cordalles and goofy Dawson Trunswick.

Spritely Grif and the stern Anuqi.

Kids—just like her—whose destinies were taken from them.

Zerif had known she would summon a Great Beast. He had never respected her. She was just another fool in one of his traps. Except more pathetic than anyone else, because she had stood by his side the entire time. She had aided the man who was taking her spirit animal and stealing her identity.

It was too late to be sorry, but that didn't stop her. Raisha wailed in despair.

And then the emotion was gone.

No longer aware of the tears on her cheeks, arcane whispers caressed the remnants of her mind. Sensing a comforting presence, she turned her head and her eyes found Zerif, her heart swelling with primal devotion. As the unearthly whispers intensified, her vision faded to blackness.

Brandon Mull is the #1 *New York Times* bestselling author of the *Fablehaven, Beyonders*, and *Five Kingdoms* series. He kicked off the Spirit Animals series with Book One: *Wild Born*, and contributed a short story in the Spirit Animals special edition: *Tales of the Great Beasts*. As a kid, he had a dog, a cat, a horse, some goldfish (won at a school carnival), and briefly a tarantula (captured in his neighborhood). He now lives in Utah with his wife, four kids, and the family dog. He thinks his spirit animal would be a dolphin.

BOOK THREE:

THE RETURN

Split between two worlds, the team races to stop an ancient evil. Above, Abeke and Rollan infiltrate an impenetrable fortress to rescue the Great Beast within, while below, Meilin and Conor find themselves adrift in a vast underground ocean.

scholastic.com/spiritanimals

Discover You

Read the Books. Play the Game.

SCHOLASTIC

scholastic.com/SpiritAnimals